MASTER OF
OBSIDIAN

MASTER OF OBSIDIAN

...Gideon handled the axe with a nonchalant ease that gave no indication how heavy the weapon really was. It swung slightly from his fingers as he edged forward, forcing Jesse to retreat until he felt the cold wall of the building at his back. "You don't find me even a little bit threatening, Jess? And be honest now." He leaned in conspiratorially. "Because I'll know if you're lying."

Jesse's stomach dropped. He remembered how frightened he had been of Gideon in the beginning, but he had let that fear go—mostly. Oddly, it wasn't the fact that Gideon was a vampire that left his palms clammy and his heart thudding. He was more aware of Gideon's basic masculinity than anything else. "A little."

The smirk returned. "A little is good." Gideon lifted a hand and rested it, palm flat, against the wall by Jesse's ear. "A little keeps you on your toes. Unless it's not your toes you're interested in being on."

Jesse was so distracted by the fact he was thoroughly trapped that it took a few seconds for the meaning of Gideon's words to sink in. Swallowing audibly, he murmured, "I don't know what you're talking about."

"See, now, I think you do. Smart guy like you, you don't really need it all spelled out for you, do you?"

And there it was. The definite press of Gideon's hips against his. The hard outline of a thick cock beneath thin trousers. The heat of the alley didn't seem nearly as bad as the heat that suddenly shot through Jesse's groin...

ALSO BY JAMIE CRAIG

Unveiled

MASTER OF OBSIDIAN

BY

JAMIE CRAIG

AMBER QUILL PRESS, LLC
http://www.amberquill.com

MASTER OF OBSIDIAN
AN AMBER QUILL PRESS BOOK

Amber Quill Press, LLC
http://www.amberquill.com
http://www.amberheat.com

Layout and Formatting provided by: ElementalAlchemy.com

PUBLISHED IN THE UNITED STATES OF AMERICA

CHAPTER 1

Jesse watched with a small, secret smile as the vampire paced around the office. He knew Gideon's frustration at being trapped in the room wasn't amusing—and Gideon would be very annoyed if he knew that Jesse was privately laughing at him—but he couldn't help it. Gideon went through the same dance of impatience and frustration every single day, almost as if he forgot his rather lethal allergy to the sun every morning, only to be rudely reminded when he stepped out for the newspaper.

Gideon would want to leave the second the sun was low enough, so Jesse knew he needed to have his research done, his maps prepared, and his notes in order. He didn't have time to watch his boss, or note the way the tension made his broad shoulders tight, or the way his dark hair flopped over his forehead. But his strong hands, clenching and unclenching into fists, kept drawing Jesse's eye. He had nice hands.

Gideon disappeared from Jesse's line of sight, allowing him to get back to his work. The case they were working on finally had a warm trail, and that was why Gideon was chomping at the bit. In the two years since Jesse had found himself thrown into Gideon's world, this was the most high-profile investigation they had conducted. Toby Richards, Councilman Richards' only son, had been found rather brutally murdered, and while it seemed most of the Chicago police force had been assigned to the case, it only took one glance at the savaged body to know it was demon-related.

And there was only one investigator in the city capable of finding the demon culprits responsible.

"We're leaving in ten minutes," Gideon warned, his voice drifting from the next room.

"I'll be ready," Jesse called back, though that was unnecessary. Of course, he'd be ready. That was his job. The most bizarre job Jesse had ever held, but his job, all the same.

Jesse closed his books and began packing his leather case. It always annoyed Gideon when he brought anything that wasn't a weapon, but having easy access to his research had saved their asses more than once. Gideon never complained anymore.

"Ready?" Gideon asked, not bothering to check if Jesse answered in the affirmative before heading to the garage.

Jesse fell in step behind his boss and friend, noticing that Gideon's pants were tighter than usual. He mentally kept a running tally of Gideon's appearance, noting slight variations and differences on a daily basis. That wasn't technically part of his job at Gideon Investigations, but he still did so faithfully. Gideon had barely changed since the day they formally met, of course, but that didn't really matter. Jesse thought he was perfect as he was.

"This is recon," Gideon said as Jesse buckled his safety belt.

"Right."

"I want you to keep an eye on the perimeter while I go into the warehouse."

"Right."

"But if you see anybody, shout for me. Don't try to—"

"To engage them. Yes, Gideon, I know."

"Good."

It wasn't that Jesse couldn't hold his own in a fair fight, but demons and vampires rarely fought fair.

He didn't need to give Gideon directions from the maps he brought. Jesse wasn't sure exactly how long Gideon had been in Chicago, though there was evidence that it was since at least before the first fire. Gideon didn't like to volunteer information about his past. Jesse wasn't sure if that was because he didn't like to dwell on the atrocities he had spent the last forty years trying to put behind him, or if he had some other inexplicable reason. One day, he hoped Gideon would assuage his curiosity, but until then, Jesse was happy with the information he had.

Jess never pried, though his life had been devoted to information and knowledge, and Gideon was a repository of history, and the stories he could tell almost made Jesse drool. But the man had given him a job when Jesse desperately needed one, and later, somehow, he had become a close friend. And Jesse firmly believed it was wrong to interrogate close friends—no matter how tempting.

There were several things Jesse avoided doing because Gideon was a close friend. He never got Gideon drunk with the ultimate goal of seducing him. He never tried to angle an invitation to his bed. He never kissed him, even when he thought Gideon sorely needed the contact. He never took advantage of the number of times Gideon sat before him, stripped naked, bleeding, and in need of first aid and a sympathetic ear to vent his frustrations. It was true he wanted to do all those things, but at the same time, he was content with the role in Gideon's life—existence—that he did have. It was a privileged one.

"There's something about this case I don't like," Gideon muttered.

"Just one thing?"

"I don't think people are being straight with us."

Jesse shrugged. That was the way of things. People obscured details, hid facts, and forgot particulars all the time. It wasn't necessarily malicious, though Gideon had the tendency to take it personally. It was their job to compensate for that and find the answers they were looking for anyway.

"Who's not being straight with us?" Jesse asked.

It was Gideon's turn to shrug. That didn't mean he didn't know; it meant he wasn't ready to talk to Jesse about it. It was a simple, familiar gesture. It was always the simple, familiar gestures that made him feel warm with appreciation, made his heart feel a little funny.

Jesse never thought he'd fall in love with a vampire. More than that, he never thought he'd fall in love with a man like Gideon. But apparently, that was the way of things, too.

When they reached the warehouse, the surrounding block was still crawling with people. Gideon growled with frustration. Jesse might have reminded him they were going to a very populated, busy industrial area before they left, but it wouldn't have done any good. Gideon wanted to be out, and nothing would have kept him indoors after the sun went down.

"We could do a bit of old-fashioned detective work," Jesse suggested.

"Meaning?"

"Ask some of these fine people if they saw anybody matching Toby's description in this area."

Gideon nodded. "That might not be a bad idea."

"If you had thought of it, you would have called it a great idea."
Gideon only grinned.

*   *   *

Four hours later, Jesse prowled through an alley alone. He wasn't sure how they'd gotten separated. It seemed one second he'd been trailing Gideon through the long alley, alternately passing through shadows and green neon lights, and the next, he'd been utterly alone. Gideon had most likely heard a demon, or sensed another vampire, or was distracted by some damsel in need of rescuing, but that didn't ease Jesse's nerves.

Jesse lifted his head, scanning the high roofs for any sign of the vampire, but there was nothing. Just more blackness. He wiped the sweat from his eyes, wishing he had a large bottle of iced water. Brown clouds hung low in the sky, almost close enough to touch.

A soft thud behind him caught his attention, and he whirled around, eyes wide, axe raised overhead. Gideon stood feet away, his lips pulling into a smirk.

"Oh, Gideon." Jesse lowered the axe. "You startled me."

"Which is why I'm over here and you're over there with the big, pointy weapon," came the amused response. With long, sinuous strides, Gideon returned to his side and reached out to take the axe, his cool fingers brushing along Jesse's. "Don't worry. You'll get it back when there's a real threat."

Jesse nervously pushed his glasses up his nose, doing his best not to notice that Gideon was standing too close, invading his personal space. "A real threat? Is the area clear of...of demons?"

"I'm still here, aren't I?"

Jesse chuckled. "Well, of course, I meant demons that are a...a threat." Gideon's eyes were inscrutable in the darkness, but he still looked vaguely amused. Jess took a half-step back, seeking some breathing room.

"Now I think I'm a little insulted here." Gideon handled the axe with a nonchalant ease that gave no indication how heavy the weapon really was. It swung slightly from his fingers as he edged forward, forcing Jesse to retreat until he felt the cold wall of the building at his back. "You don't find me even a little bit threatening, Jess? And be honest now." He leaned in conspiratorially. "Because I'll know if you're lying."

4

Jesse's stomach dropped. He remembered how frightened he had been of Gideon in the beginning, but he had let that fear go—mostly. Oddly, it wasn't the fact that Gideon was a vampire that left his palms clammy and his heart thudding. He was more aware of Gideon's basic masculinity than anything else. "A little."

The smirk returned. "A little is good." Gideon lifted a hand and rested it, palm flat, against the wall by Jesse's ear. "A little keeps you on your toes. Unless it's not your toes you're interested in being on."

Jesse was so distracted by the fact he was thoroughly trapped that it took a few seconds for the meaning of Gideon's words to sink in. Swallowing audibly, he murmured, "I don't know what you're talking about."

"See, now, I think you do. Smart guy like you, you don't really need it all spelled out for you, do you?"

And there it was. The definite press of Gideon's hips against his. The hard outline of a thick cock beneath thin trousers. The heat of the alley didn't seem nearly as bad as the heat that suddenly shot through Jesse's groin.

Gideon's nostrils flared, and Jesse knew he didn't have a chance at bluffing his way through this, or playing dumb. Questions he'd long suppressed came to the surface of his mind. What did Gideon taste like? What did he feel like? What did he smell like? What the hell was going on in Gideon's mind? Why this? Why now? Did Gideon see these questions reflected on his face?

"Maybe I do."

For long seconds, Gideon merely gazed at him. The night shadowed his eyes from Jesse's careful scrutiny, but the twitch in his jaw and the continued flare of his nostrils sent a dark thrill through Jess' veins.

"And who would've thought that *need* and *want* meant the same thing to Jesse Madding," Gideon murmured. "You want it spelled out for you? Let's start with A. For arousal."

The axe clattered to the ground as Gideon tossed it aside, and the hand that had gripped the handle so assuredly was suddenly around Jesse's wrist. Hard enough to border on pain. Immovable.

Without looking away, Gideon guided Jesse's hand to their pressed hips. He inched back enough to allow his fingers to come to rest on Gideon's waistband. "Take me out," he ordered.

Jesse's heart slammed against his chest, and he didn't know if the weight settling in his lower stomach was fear or relief—relief seemed most likely. His fingers were awkward at first, numb and slick with sweat, but he forced himself to concentrate. He worked the zipper down and reached into Gideon's tight pants to grasp his hard, smooth shaft. Jesse pulled him from the material, gripping him loosely, and looked up with questioning eyes, trying to suppress his excitement. He didn't want to look like an over-eager puppy.

The smile that greeted him reminded Jess of some of the pictures in his father's books, the ones that were kept under lock and key in the back of the cupboard Jess was never supposed to have seen. He had, though. He had been far too curious to restrain himself, and the memory of the devils, smiling over the seething bodies at their feet, superimposed over Gideon's features for a moment long enough to make Jesse's cock jump.

"That wasn't hard, now was it?" Gideon taunted. A soft chuckle filled the space between them. "Except I am. And do you know why, Jess?"

Jesse shook his head mutely. He couldn't form any words, his throat too constricted to allow that much air to pass. He moved his wrist without thought, stroking Gideon's cock from the bottom to the top and then back again.

Something hard glinted in Gideon's eye, and the grip around Jesse's wrist tightened. "I asked you a question. I expect you to use your mouth to form all those pretty words you like so much."

Jesse's cock jumped again. "I…no. No, I don't know why, Gideon."

He leaned in as if he was going to kiss him. At the last minute, Gideon turned his head and skimmed his mouth over Jesse's cheek until it settled over his ear.

"Because I see you. I see the way you look at me. Do you have any idea how *hungry* you look?" Jess shivered as Gideon snaked his tongue out and traced along his lobe. "Do you have any idea how hungry that makes *me*?"

Jesse was suddenly very, *very* aware of how close Gideon's mouth was to his neck, and how delicate his skin was. A hint of fear skittered down his spine, but that was far from the strongest reaction Gideon was pulling from him. He shook his head, but remembered Gideon wanted him to speak, and murmured, "I…I didn't know."

"You didn't know that I dream about sinking into you? Or didn't know that when you look at me, you clench your ass every single time?"

There was no sense in denying he had a strong physical reaction to Gideon—though he wouldn't characterize it as *every* time. "I didn't know you dream about me."

"And why wouldn't I?" The hand around Jesse's wrist disappeared, only to reappear at his belt. Jesse didn't feel Gideon's light fingers as he undid the buckle and opened up his pants to free his aching cock. "You walk around the office with a hard-on. You look at me like a puppy desperate to be petted." Jess gasped as Gideon stroked once, hard, up his length. "And you make that gorgeous O shape with your mouth that's just begging to be filled. Tell me how I'm supposed to resist."

Jesse licked his dry lips, but it didn't seem to help. Gideon followed the small gesture with his eyes. He didn't know how to respond to that, though he suspected Gideon still wanted him to speak. As his glasses slid down his slick nose, he shook his head.

Pulling back, Gideon clicked his tongue. "Someone's not learning his lessons."

He stepped back without warning, and Jesse nearly stumbled forward. Gideon caught him with a strong hand around the back of his neck, and the next thing Jess knew he was being forced to his knees.

"Time for the letter B," Gideon said. "And pardon me for being crude here, but…hell, why am I apologizing? Blow."

It wouldn't occur to Jesse to resist, even if Gideon couldn't break his neck with a twist of his wrist. Gideon's commanding tone didn't leave any room for denial. He trembled as he opened his mouth and leaned forward, closing his lips around Gideon's cock. The second the cool, velvety skin touched his tongue, Jesse moaned. Gideon increased the pressure on his neck, forcing him to relax his jaw and swallow Gideon's cock to the root.

"That's it." Gideon sighed. He held him in place as his other hand came up to stroke the hollow of Jesse's cheek, a gesture almost frightening in its gentleness. "You feel fucking amazing, Jess, but I knew you would. You don't do anything halfway."

Jesse wanted to return the sentiment. Gideon felt more than amazing. He rolled his tongue around Gideon's shaft, waiting for the implicit, or explicit, permission to move again. He closed his eyes, savoring the way Gideon tasted, the way he completely filled Jesse's mouth. He looked up to Gideon through his eyelashes, waiting.

The grip at the back of his neck loosened but didn't entirely disappear. "Suck me," Gideon said. The hoarseness of his voice surprised Jess; perhaps he wasn't the only one treading on thin ice here. "And think of it this way. You want me good and wet because I didn't

Boy Scout and bring any lube with me."

Jesse's chest burned. Gideon's dark promise had stolen the air from his lungs. He took a deep breath through his nose as he pulled back, dragging Gideon's heavy cock through his lips. He gripped Gideon's hips with both hands, and then began bobbing his head. Hollowing his cheeks, he created as much suction as he could with each stroke.

The muscles flexed beneath his palms, the flesh cool and hard as he molded his fingers over it. Every time Jess sank down Gideon's length, Gideon clenched his ass. If Jess had been a little bolder—or didn't have his mouth full—he might have commented that maybe Gideon was the one eager to get fucked.

Of course, that would undoubtedly compel Gideon to fuck him even sooner. Jesse suddenly wished it was possible to speak and suck at the same time.

Jesse slipped his fingers between Gideon's thighs, cupping his balls gently. He rolled them around his fingers, weighing them, massaging them. Gideon widened his legs more, but he wasn't making a single sound. Jesse needed to hear something, anything, any sign that he was doing the right thing, doing it the right way. He redoubled his efforts, letting the tip of Gideon's cock go down his throat, pausing, sliding back slowly, and then swallowing it just as deeply, again and again.

It started with the smallest of grunts.

Jess wasn't even sure he'd heard correctly, so focused was he on savoring every inch of Gideon's cock. But then it came again, a little louder this time, and Gideon's hips thrust forward slightly to meet his downstroke.

Jess took courage in that. On a whim, he scratched his fingernails along the sensitive skin of Gideon's sac. The jolt that drove the cock deep into Jesse's throat prompted him to do it again, and soon enough, the words of encouragement were spilling from Gideon's lips.

"Made for this, weren't you?" he said. "I'll bet you were a hit with all those English schoolboys. Probably earned your grades on your knees with your mouth wrapped around their...oh *fuck*." A shudder rippled through Gideon. "Fucking love your mouth, Jess. You need a new job in the office. On your knees, under my desk, worshiping my cock. Bet you'd fucking love that. I know I would. Fuck, yeah, just like that."

Jesse paused long enough to nod. His cock throbbed, the pleasure-pain focused in his groin and radiating through his body. He felt it everywhere from his toes to his back teeth. He wanted to come, he felt like if Gideon kept talking he *would* come, but he didn't dare try to relieve some of the pressure. That would require taking attention away from Gideon, and he didn't have to be told that wasn't acceptable.

The hold on the back of his neck began to tighten, Gideon's answering thrusts growing increasingly erratic. When Jesse felt Gideon's balls tense, he almost smiled in anticipation of the taste about to erupt along his tongue. But then Gideon was jerking back his head, and wrapping his own hand around his cock, and all Jesse could do was watch as Gideon stroked once, twice, and then came with a roar, his warm come shooting out to splash on Jesse's face.

Jesse nearly whimpered, his cock twitching and jerking, like it was being tugged on a string. He put his tongue out, licking a drop of come from his cheek as it rolled down his face. He put a hand up to wipe it away, but Gideon caught his wrist, a simple shake of his head enough to stop him. "Gideon…" Jesse didn't mean it to happen, but it came out as an almost desperate plea.

Gideon used his hold to pull Jess back to his feet. "I didn't think it was possible," he said. "But you look even more delicious."

He leaned in and licked a path along Jesse's cheek. Before Jess made a sound, Gideon sealed their mouths together, his come-coated tongue thrusting inside.

Jesse sucked Gideon's tongue into his mouth like he sucked Gideon's cock, eagerly capturing every drop that had been denied him. He was overheated, flushed, and he knew it had nothing to do with the summer night's humidity. Jesse's hand snuck up to hold the back of Gideon's head, his fingers curling into Gideon's skin.

The hard kiss slowed, deepened, shifted into something languorous that made the earth feel like it was pitching beneath his feet. His lungs were burning by the time Gideon pulled away, but he didn't let go of his hold. He wouldn't until Gideon made him.

Dark eyes flickered over Jesse's face. "I'm going to let you go now. But you're not going to run, not that I think you would anyway. You're going to step back, and you're going to strip, and you're not going to even *think* about wiping off my come, because if you do, I'm going to walk away and I will never touch you again. Do you understand, Jess?"

"Yes, I understand."

Gideon's hand fell away, and Jesse took a step back, pushing his pants down without a second thought. A part of him knew they were in the middle of an alley and anybody or anything might stumble upon them, and that part was mortifying. But the rest of him didn't even acknowledge that fact. His pants went to his ankles, and he unbuttoned his shirt slowly with trembling fingers. Once the buttons were free, he tossed it to the ground.

Gideon didn't move until the last of Jesse's clothing was gone and he stood there, shivering, exposed, waiting for the next command. He watched Gideon drop his hand to his cock, and his mouth watered when he saw it was still hard, a fresh drop of fluid already collecting at the tip. By the time he was able to tear his hungry gaze away from it, Gideon's human visage was gone.

The vampire, fanged and dangerous, grinned back at him.

"I think I'd like another kiss."

He prowled forward, and Jess retreated on instinct, only to be jerked to a halt by Gideon's powerful hand on his shoulder. Gideon closed the distance between them, and when the hand that had been stroking his cock suddenly engulfed Jesse's as well, he thought he would come on the spot. Only biting the inside of his cheek stopped that from happening.

Jesse never wanted to admit that he found the fangs, the flashing yellow eyes, the ridged brow arousing, but he did. And the toothy grin told him Gideon knew it, too. Gideon continued stroking his erection slowly, their cocks sliding against each other. As Gideon claimed his mouth again, his fangs cut into Jesse's tender lips, spilling drops of blood onto Gideon's tongue. Despite the surprising sting, Jesse didn't pull away. The pain was another double-edged sword. It served both to distract him and to amplify the desperate need that left him teetering right on the edge.

The kiss was short-lived, though Gideon seemed to spend an inordinate amount of time afterward simply tracing the curve of Jesse's lips with his tongue. "So," he said, "how many times a day do you jerk off thinking of me, Jess? Inquiring minds want to know."

"It…it depends," Jesse answered haltingly. "Two, maybe, three."

"Depends? On what?"

"On you," he admitted, unable to meet Gideon's eyes. "On what you do. On whether or not you touch me."

Gideon pressed Jesse back until he felt the harsh scrape of the wall against his skin. With his body keeping Jess in place now, he released his grip and wiped away more of the come. "And what gets you especially hot under the research book?" He released their cocks, reaching around to cup Jesse's ass, strong fingers pulling the cheeks apart as his come-sticky fingers slid around the other side to skim down the crack.

Jesse tensed at the first brush of contact, but the flash of warning on Gideon's face forced him to relax. He didn't know how to answer the question. Didn't Gideon understand there wasn't any one thing that prompted a physical reaction?

"The casual contact," Jesse said breathlessly. "When you don't realize you're touching me, or when you do realize it, but you don't care. Or...or when you come back to your apartment, and you strip on your way to the shower, and I want to..." Jesse's voice failed as Gideon pushed one finger into his ass.

"You want to what?"

When an answer wasn't forthcoming—because really, why the hell did Gideon think he could *speak* when he was about to burst from getting fucked with a finger?—Gideon growled and shoved him into the wall. Jesse's head snapped back, eyes wide as he met Gideon's, and he groaned as Gideon crooked his finger and went in deliberate search of his prostate.

"I asked you a question," Gideon said. "And if you don't answer it, I'm going to spread you as wide as you go and fuck you now. No more stretching, no more lube." His golden eyes glittered. "Unless that's what you really do want, in which case I'm more than happy to oblige."

Jesse knew that if Gideon followed through with his threat—promise—he probably wouldn't be able to walk the next day, or even the day after. Or sit for any length of time. But it seemed like every inch of him, inside and out, was shouting for Gideon, desperate for more. He had been hoping for this for so long, fantasizing about it. He thought if he had to wait another second, he'd shatter.

"Gideon...fuck me...please..."

For a moment, disbelief shone in Gideon's eyes. It quickly disappeared, though, to be replaced by an awed lust that had him moving, withdrawing his hand from Jesse's ass and grasping each cheek to lift him off the ground. Gideon hefted him high enough for Jess to wrap his legs around Gideon's hips, and then—somehow—pulled his flesh even farther apart until he felt more exposed than he'd ever been before.

"You're going to make a great little cockslut," Gideon murmured. He angled his hips to press the blunt tip of his cock against Jesse's hole. "Now...what was that you wanted?"

"Fuck me," Jesse panted. "Gideon...I need you..."

Gideon pushed forward until he breached the tight outer ring. Then he stopped and tilted his head. "You know what? I don't think I heard the magic word."

The sudden pressure was nearly his undoing. He knew once he started talking, he wasn't going to be able to stop. The words would fall out of his mouth with each breath. "Please, Gideon, please, please…"

"Yeah," Gideon muttered. "You're going to be a fucking fantastic little slut for me." His mouth skimmed over Jesse's, his fangs nicking the lower lip. "Now buckle up. We're about to go for a ride."

Jesse half-expected Gideon to slam inside of him in one, long stroke. It would be excruciating, and it would likely leave him useless for days, but considering Gideon's mood, it made the most sense.

He didn't expect the slow, almost deliberate thrust. He didn't expect to feel every single centimeter of Gideon's thick cock as it forced its way into his passage. And he definitely didn't expect to start trembling long before Gideon was fully sheathed.

"I can just imagine it," Gideon was saying. They were whispers, actually, and when Gideon had moved his mouth to his ear, Jess had no idea. "The office is going to be a hell of a lot more interesting from this point out, that's for sure."

Jesse hoped Gideon didn't expect an answer, because he had none, not even a moan. He nodded frantically, agreeing with every word that Gideon said. He clenched tightly around Gideon's cock, but Gideon barely allowed him time to adjust before rocking out and then pushing forward again. And each time Gideon thrust forward, Jesse saw stars erupt before his eyes.

The descriptions of what Gideon was going to do to him, on his desk, under his desk, against the wall, soon disintegrated into murmurings of *so tight* and *could fuck you all night* and *wanted this for so long*, all accompanied by ever-more-forceful pounds into his ass. It was the last that made Jesse squeeze his eyes shut, and when Gideon licked a path down his neck to suck hard at his pulse point, Jesse didn't resist tilting his head to the side.

A growl rumbled through Gideon's chest. The moment Jesse felt the fangs sink through his skin, Gideon wrapped a hand around his cock and pumped once down its length with an iron grip.

Gideon's cock, Gideon's teeth, Gideon's firm grasp around his shaft, were all too much. As Gideon dragged the first mouthful of blood from his neck, Jesse erupted in his hand, coming in several long spurts that coated his stomach and chest. He didn't know what to expect from Gideon, but it wasn't the deepening of his fangs, or a longer pull of blood. His ass clenched convulsively around Gideon and he grew increasingly light-headed. And Gideon kept drinking. A brief flare of panic was replaced by a distant sense of euphoria as he clung tighter to Gideon's strong shoulders.

Vaguely, he became aware of the stiffening of Gideon's body, the violent slams into his ass as Gideon shot again and again. He didn't have the strength to fight against him, and even less desire, but as he felt the world begin to darken around the edges, the hard pull through his veins disappeared, and Gideon's mouth was on his, his bloody tongue forcing its way past Jesse's lips to twist and tangle with his.

The coppery taste of his own blood shocked Jesse's system, and his head jerked back, but Gideon wouldn't let him pull away. He forced Jess to taste every inch of his hot tongue as he explored every part of Jesse's mouth. Gideon's body felt almost feverish now, full of stolen warmth, and the world darkened around the edges again as Gideon refused to let him pause for a breath. His lungs felt like they were going to explode before Gideon yanked his head away, and Jesse gasped for breath that barely made a difference.

"Do you know how tempted I am?" Gideon murmured. "I could kill you right now and you wouldn't be able to do a single thing to stop me. Or I could turn you, and again, I *really* don't think you'd stop me."

His features shifted, and the familiar brown eyes gazed at Jess, burning more brightly somehow than his golden eyes had. "But I'm not going to." He shifted his weight so that his cock, still buried balls deep in Jesse's ass, brushed against Jesse's prostate. "And do you know why?" He began licking away the last remnants of his drying come from Jesse's face, each swipe almost a caress as it soothed and cleaned his skin. "Because you are way too delicious this way, Jess. All warm and hungry and so fucking greedy for it."

As Gideon spoke, Jesse knew he meant it, and once again, he felt that curious combination of fear and arousal. He rested against Gideon's body, his eyes closed, enjoying every inch, every moment of contact.

"I am," he murmured. "Greedy for it. Want you all the time." Even the simple words were too much of a burden on his over-taxed system, and now concern pierced the dense fog that had shrouded his mind. How was he going to dress himself? How was he going to get himself home? Did he have a death wish, letting Gideon bite him like that? Was there something wrong with him? Because he knew for a fact he'd let Gideon do it again.

"Let's get you home." The soft command was at odds with Gideon's earlier force, and he set Jesse down, leaning him against the wall as he gathered up his clothes. The hands that dressed him were gentle and strong, and when he was done, Gideon pulled Jess back into his arms. "All the time might as well start now."

CHAPTER 2

Gideon woke feeling warmer and more sated than he had in a very long time. His flesh still hummed from the rush of stolen blood, and the scent of sex hung so heavily in the air that his cock began to thicken before he opened his eyes. It helped, too, that the hard body he was currently wrapped around reeked of blood and his come. Without thinking, he bent and buried his face in his bedmate's neck, sucking lightly at the puncture wounds his tongue found.

It was the soft groan that finally cut through Gideon's morning fog. A groan he recognized all too well. The only difference was, he'd only ever heard it as a pained sound before. This was entirely new. But the throat it came from wasn't.

Jess.

God, it was *Jess*.

The memories of the previous night came slamming back in a scarlet gale that had Gideon flying from the bed, staring down at his best friend's supine form stretched out along his sheets. *His* bed. Gideon's. Where Jess had never been before. Where he'd always sworn Jess would never be, because fuck if Gideon was going to mess up the best relationship of his existence with something as messy as sex.

But he had. And he'd done it in a dirty alley with little regard to Jesse's feelings and all his attention on his own pleasure. For some inexplicable reason, he'd tossed away every iota of decency and respect he had for Jess in favor of forcing the man to bend to his desires. Reliving the memories made him fully hard, but it didn't stop the shame from pushing him farther away from the bed.

Jesse's eyes fluttered open. Bright blue burned into Gideon's, and a small smile curved the mouth he remembered all too well wrapped around his cock. Before he let Jess speak, however, Gideon held up his hands, palms out, in apology.

"I am so sorry about last night," he said.

Jesse blinked and sat up, but his body swayed like supporting his own weight was too much of an effort, and he relaxed against the pillows once again. Gideon braced himself for a withering look of disappointment, or a lecture, or, God, an apology. He imagined Jesse fumbling all over himself, trying to explain that it was his own very existence that was the problem, not anything Gideon did.

But he merely whispered, "I'm not."

Gideon froze. "What're you talking about? I almost *killed* you, Jess. That's not…that isn't…" His impotent frustration choked the words off in his throat. Some days he shouldn't bother getting up.

"Can I have some water?" Jesse rasped. "My throat is a little sore."

Scowling at his own inconsideration, Gideon took long strides from the bedroom to the kitchen, trying not to think about why Jesse's throat was sore, or how good it had felt filling it with his cock. The water splashed over the sides of the glass as he hurried back, fresh apologies already on his tongue as he handed it over.

Of course, it would be better if the memory of those minutes in the alley didn't give him a raging hard-on. Or if Jess didn't look at it over the rim of his glass as he sipped at the water like he wished it was that in his mouth instead.

"But you didn't," Jesse said, once he drained most of the glass. Gideon looked at him blankly. "Kill me. You didn't kill me, even though we both know you could have at any time."

"That doesn't make it right." He backed up, turning on his heel as he looked around for his pants. He found them lying forgotten next to Jesse's shredded shirt. Fuck. He'd forgotten ripping the clothes off Jess when they got back to his apartment. "I don't know what got into me," Gideon continued. "I'm not…I wouldn't treat you like that."

"I know you wouldn't." Jesse set the glass aside. "Which are you more upset about? That we…had sex or the way we had sex?"

"That wasn't sex." He stabbed his legs into his pants, jerking them up around his hips. "That was me taking advantage of you for my own gratification."

A shadow passed over Jesse's eyes. "You weren't taking advantage of me, Gideon. I can see why you'd think that, since you're stronger than me, but you didn't make me do anything I didn't *want* to do."

Somehow, hearing that only made feel Gideon worse. As unleashed as he'd been in the alley, it wasn't that far off from how he knew he could get in sexual encounters. He liked being in control, he got off knowing he was the one in charge. And he knew many of his observations about Jess had been accurate. He would have to be blind not to see how Jesse looked at him when he thought Gideon wouldn't notice, and having enhanced senses weren't necessary to see the erections Jess commonly sported. Jess wanted it, all right, but only because he'd been attracted to Gideon for months.

That wasn't good enough for Gideon.

"Look," he tried again. He felt a little braver with his cock covered, though the way Jesse's gaze kept straying, he knew his arousal was still far too evident. "Last night shouldn't have happened. Maybe you did want me to...do what I did, but I know and you know that's only because there's this physical attraction between us. And I'm not going to fuck up our friendship by turning you into my sex slave, there to satisfy my every whim. You deserve better than that, Jess."

Gideon watched the wheels spinning in Jesse's head. For a moment, Gideon thought Jess planned to argue with him, but that moment passed. "I see," Jesse said stiffly, swinging his legs over the side of the bed. "You're right, of course. Our friendship is more important. Not to mention our professional relationship."

He exhaled in relief. "Exactly." He smiled, trying to lighten the mood. "I mean, really, how much work are we going to get done if you spend all your time on your knees?"

"We'd have to learn how to multi-task, and I know how much you hate that," Jesse said, pushing the sheets aside shamelessly.

Gideon's eyes widened. Jesse had more than a few teeth marks marring his body. He looked like...well, he looked like somebody who had spent all night in bed with a vampire. A vampire who wasn't terribly concerned if his bedmate was entirely conscious.

"Gideon? I'd like to take a shower, but I'm afraid I don't have anything to wear."

"You can borrow something of mine," he replied automatically. "But maybe you should spend today in bed. You had a...rough night."

Jesse rubbed his cheek. "I'd like to wash up a bit, at least."

His gaze was fixed on the spot Jess was worrying with his fingertips. It was already going rough with stubble, but through the dark hairs, Gideon noticed the tiny flecks of dried come clinging to his skin. His mouth watered.

"Stay there."

The only thing disappearing to the kitchen did was make the scent less prevalent. As Gideon filled a basin with steaming hot water, he bowed his head, trying to banish every thought of how Jess had tasted, how Jess had writhed, how Jess had begged Gideon to let him come in the wee hours of the morning when not even the stars were out to play. By the time he returned to the bedroom, all he'd accomplished was thickening his layers of guilt.

Jess should have better, but it had been so long since Gideon had had somebody in his life he could call his best friend, he had forgotten there were certain lines not to be crossed if one didn't want to lose said best friend.

And Gideon couldn't lose Jesse. He needed the man far too much for that.

Jesse sat patiently while Gideon set about the task of bathing him. He tried to tell himself it wasn't any different than the simple first aid tasks Jesse performed on a nearly nightly basis, but it was different. For starters, there was the unmistakably fresh smell of Jesse's arousal. And despite the multiple bite wounds, there wasn't a single drop of blood on Jesse's skin. Gideon had seen to that before they both passed out in exhaustion.

"Gideon, I know you're going to be wrapped up in your guilt for quite some time, but I wish you wouldn't. I don't regret last night. I'm not sorry it happened. If you don't want it to happen again, I understand. But don't...brood over it."

Gideon frowned, ducking his head to avoid Jesse's steady gaze. "I'm not brooding."

"Maybe not right this second, but you're close. And I'm sure when you're finished here, you'll go upstairs to the office, turn off the light, pull the shades, and mull over every single detail."

Sometimes he hated how well Jesse knew him.

"I'm going to pull the fucking shades because it's the middle of the day. And I'm not going to mull." At least, he was going to do his damnedest not to. "I'm going to find out what the hell happened to me last night before it happens again and I turn you into a chew toy."

Jesse looked pointedly at his chest. "I think it might be a little late for that, but I appreciate the sentiment." He lifted his chin, exposing his neck, making himself vulnerable. "Be sure to get under my chin, too. I feel a little...itchy."

Gideon's fingers tightened around the washcloth. Taking Jesse's chin in hand, he tilted the other man's head to the side to avoid his eyes before setting the damp cloth to his skin. Both of them knew there wasn't anything there, but Gideon's first mark, the one he'd felt searing all the way to his toes, the one he'd had to struggle to pull away from because Jesse's blood had been so fucking succulent, lay within two inches of where Gideon washed, begging him to return and take a taste.

"You need somebody who's not going to hurt you," he heard himself saying.

"Some things hurt more than others, Gideon."

There was nothing to say to that. Jesse's desire was unmistakable. But Gideon's resolve was stronger.

Dropping the cloth back into the basin, Gideon rose from the bed and crossed to his wardrobe. "I'll leave my cell phone on the nightstand for you," he said. He began pulling out clothes he thought might fit Jess, heedless of the color or match. They were about the same height, but his broader frame meant most of his shirts would hang on Jesse's leaner form. "If you need anything, you call me, all right?"

"I was doing some research last night before we went out. If you could bring me my books? They're upstairs. Oh, and maybe you should write down what happened last night?" Jesse frowned and shook his head. "I mean, what happened to you when we were separated. Maybe you unknowingly ran into the creature we're looking for."

"Books. Check. But I can tell you what creatures I ran into. None. I thought I heard something in that warehouse, so I ducked inside to check it out. Came out on the roof, jumped down into the alley, and..." His voice trailed off. They both knew very well what happened next.

Jesse nodded. "Right. Well, maybe we can investigate the warehouse again later."

The last thing Gideon wanted was for Jess to be anywhere near the warehouse. "I'll check with Richards to see if the location means anything to him. He's the one who pointed us to that neighborhood in the first place. Maybe there's a link between what happened to me and what happened to his son."

"What did happen to you, Gideon? I mean...I know what *happened*, but what did it feel like? Was it your demon? Was it something else?"

It would be nice to be able to blame his actions on the fact that he was a vampire. It would be a lot easier to look Jesse in the eye if Gideon could say, "Yeah, that damn demon. It's all his fault." But it would be a lie, and for as much damage as Gideon was sure he'd already done to their friendship, the last thing he needed was to add dishonesty to the list of his crimes.

"That was all me," he conceded. He stuck his nose in his wardrobe to look for a shirt for himself, unable to meet Jesse's inquisitive gaze. "I just…didn't care about consequences. I knew what I wanted and I was going to take it." The rest of it came out in a rush. "And being in charge makes it hotter."

"I figured it was probably all you," Jesse said softly. "I doubt your demon would have let me crawl away from a meeting like that. Although, I do hope you don't truly believe that I made it through school on my knees. Because I didn't."

"No, no, of course not. You're too smart for that." Curiosity got the better of him. "But last night wasn't the first time you've given a blow job. At least, if it was, you're not only smart, but the fastest study I've ever known." Or a born natural, he thought, but kept it to himself.

"No, it wasn't my first time," Jesse said mildly. "You're not the first man I…" He almost visibly called back his words, substituting them with, "have been physically attracted to."

He had to know. "Please tell me it wasn't your first time getting fucked, either. Because if I thought that was all you had to base the experience on…"

"You'd what? Take it back? Give me something else to compare it to?"

His cock jumped at the thought of fucking Jess properly. On his back, on his bed, maybe spreadeagle and cuffed and taking the time to pound into his ass for hours…

Gideon swallowed against the wave of lust. "I'd never forgive myself," he ground out.

"Oh, well. Don't let it keep you up at night. It wasn't my first time for that, either."

It was a small relief, but not nearly enough to alleviate his mood. Slipping his shirt on over his head, Gideon removed his cell phone from his pants pocket and set it on the nightstand, before hurrying to the door.

"I'll bring those books right down," he said.

He was out the door before Jess could respond. The first thing he was going to do when he got to his desk was jerk off. Maybe then he'd be able to concentrate enough to figure out what had happened to him.

CHAPTER 3

When Jesse appeared at the office door, dressed and pale, Gideon expected the worst. It would be like Jess to want to sit and dissect the night's events, down to the last minute, in order to analyze what had exactly happened. And if he pushed the topic, Gideon would have no choice but to comply. There was a reason Jess was the brains behind the operation, and in the end, they still had a case to fathom out.

It was with more than a hint of relief, then, when Jesse announced he was feeling better and going home. Gideon waved him off with warnings to take it easy, to take the next day off, and to call if he needed anything, all without rising from his seat behind the desk. Standing was a very bad idea. In spite of jerking off earlier, his cock had gotten hard the instant the scent of Jesse's blood hit his nose.

Without the distraction of knowing Jesse was within walking distance, it was easier to concentrate on the task at hand. The facts they had on the case were few, but the events at the warehouse cast a new light on them, a very dark and sinister light. Toby Richards wasn't a demon—as far as Gideon knew—but if he'd gone into the warehouse as well, perhaps some metamorphosis had transpired, something that had led to his death.

The smart thing would be to go back and check it out. All he had were impressions from his few minutes inside, and none of it was nearly concrete enough for him to give Jesse to research. There were no creatures to locate, no mysterious objects to identify. Going back by the light of day could provide better evidence about what had drawn

Gideon inside.

Except he couldn't go during the day. And the last thing he wanted was for Jesse to investigate alone. And he still had another three hours until sundown.

Gideon leaned back in his chair, his thoughts back on the man who'd spent the night in his bed. Jess wasn't sorry. Jess had seemed ready to pursue even more. Jess would probably have been attached to Gideon's dick in some way or another if he'd been the one to wake up first, and Gideon wouldn't have been able to stop him. Wouldn't have *wanted* to stop him.

He'd known about the attraction for a long time, maybe from the moment they'd met. In the beginning, before he'd come to know the man, Gideon had used it to his advantage, getting Jess to work for free with the occasional sly glance or casual flirtatious remark. But as soon as a real friendship had started to form, Gideon had stopped. It was easy to find a sexual partner any time he wanted; friends, on the other hand, were a rare and precious commodity. He'd stifled any attraction he might have for Jess, and he'd hoped Jesse had done the same, suppressing it in favor of a more meaningful relationship.

Apparently, he'd been biding his time, waiting for the right opportunity. The one Gideon had dropped into when he'd leapt back into the alley.

For a brief moment, Gideon considered it. His actions with Jess weren't out of character, just not the character he tried to present to the outside world, and certainly not the one he'd presented to his best friend. He liked his partners pliant and pleading; the more they begged, the harder Gideon got. But he didn't want to see Jess plead. He liked the man who shared his office; he respected him for his intelligence and his dry humor and the way he was willing to do whatever it took to get a job done. He honestly didn't know how Jess expected the two versions of himself to reconcile, and given the choice, there was no doubt which Gideon preferred.

Jess was his best friend. Gideon was going to make sure it stayed like that.

He glanced at the clock on the wall. Nobody would blame him if he called it a day and went back to bed, but Gideon knew doing so would invite dreams he couldn't control. They would be dark and vivid, with Jesse in a starring role, and considering his shame regarding his actions, Gideon wasn't so sure it wouldn't be him taking the sexual assault this time instead of Jess. Better to stay busy, which meant finding a new angle on the Toby Richards case to follow.

It all came back to the warehouse. Had Councilman Richards been aware of its significance and steered them in its general direction to deflect any suspicion? When Gideon had called earlier to speak with him, he hadn't been available. Perhaps it was time for another face-to-face meeting. He'd get answers and be in a better position to judge how honest the councilman was being with them.

Grabbing his coat and keys, Gideon took the stairs down to the underground parking structure where his car was. Except for a sliver on the windshield, the windows were painted black on his '73 Berlinetta Boxer in order to block out lethal rays of sunlight—a precaution he hated because it spoiled the car's sleek lines—but he'd owned his baby since Ferrari had first made it publicly available. Nostalgia and a sense of masculine pride refused him the right to trade it in for something that wasn't as flashy. He argued it away by saying that as long as the car was functional, there was no reason to replace it.

He was smiling when he hit the street. She cornered like a dream, too. Getting behind the wheel always sent a thrill of power through his veins.

He realized when he hit the traffic downtown that he'd timed it poorly. Rush hour was starting, and Gideon got stuck more than once as the streets clogged with commuters. It left him tapping at the steering wheel, trying his best to ignore the rising heat inside the vehicle. The raised temperature exacerbated the scent of Jesse's blood and come that clung to the passenger seat. Couldn't he go *anywhere* without being reminded of what had happened?

His nerves were completely frayed by the time he pulled into the dark parking structure next to the councilmen offices. Gideon was eager to escape the car and the ghosts of what he'd done the night before.

He went up the back stairs, climbing them two at a time. Gideon passed the occasional employee on the way out, obviously opting for a pseudo-cardio routine by taking the stairs instead of the elevator, but otherwise, nobody gave him a second glance. By the time he reached the fourteenth floor, the building was nearly silent around him, and he let himself into the councilman's office unseen.

Councilman Lucas Richards sat at his oversized mahogany desk, his feet propped up on the corner as he looked over a file resting in his lap. For a man in his sixties, he was remarkably trim, his hair only starting to salt-and-pepper, and the stretch of his lean body made him look taller than his normal five-seven. He looked very much like he had when Gideon had first met him thirty years earlier, all the way down to the posturing to make himself seem larger than he really was. Gideon often had the urge to explain to the man that power had nothing to do with how big you were, but held his tongue. It was too amusing to watch Lucas try to be something he wasn't.

"One of these days, you're going to learn to knock," Lucas said without looking up.

"You like me better when I don't." Gideon stood on the other side of the desk, his unsmiling eyes fixed on Richards. "We need to talk."

"I got that impression from your four messages."

"And yet, you seem more interested in pretending to be busy than in finding out what I might have learned about Toby's death. Interesting."

Mentioning Toby finally tore Lucas' gaze away from the folder, and he lifted a pale gray gaze to Gideon. "Did you find the killer?"

"If that was the case, you'd be talking to a cop right now."

His denial made Lucas sag back against his leather chair. "Then why are you bothering me, Gideon? This isn't your playground. Go bully somebody else."

Coming around the edge of the desk, Gideon perched on its corner, pushing aside Richards' resting feet with his hip. "You brought me in to do a job," he said. "But that doesn't mean you dictate how I get it done."

"You've been on this for a week without anything new. I'm beginning to wonder if I wasn't wasting my time, coming to you."

When Lucas tried turning his attention back to the file, Gideon ripped it out of his hand, tossing it to the other side of the room and out of his reach. "We're talking," he said, his voice low and clipped. "That means you listen. And then you tell me what I need to know, or I rip your throat out. Just because I can."

In spite of the threat, there was no apprehension in Lucas' gaze, no fear seeping from his pores. "I know you too well to believe that," he replied. "Your commitment to this town goes back to my grandfather's days, so trying to scare me by reminding me you're a vampire won't work. But, obviously, something has you hot under the collar, so go ahead. I'm listening."

Lucas Richards was not one of Gideon's favorite people, for a lot of reasons, but he had a point. A long time ago, Gideon had made a vow to protect and help the city, and he wasn't going to break it now. Even if he didn't like how some of its citizens behaved. But the thought of draining Lucas and tossing him aside filled him with dark glee.

"That area of town you directed me to," he said. "I need to know why you sent me there and what you expected me to discover."

The lines around Lucas' eyes deepened as he frowned. "What did you find?"

"I believe I'm asking the questions here."

Lucas stared at him, unblinking, his mouth tight as he seemed to weigh his response. "Toby got picked up in that area two weeks before we found his body," he said. "A local business had reported a break-in, and Toby matched the description. He told me it was a mistake, that he'd been lost. I pulled some strings and got the charges dropped."

"This business. What was it?"

Lucas shrugged. "I don't even remember exactly. But it doesn't matter. It was their warehouse that reported it."

And there it was. The link Gideon had been looking for. He needed to find out what that warehouse had housed. If it was capable of turning an innocent young man into some kind of beast, it needed to be stopped before the rest of the populace was put at risk.

"I want a copy of the police report," he said. "You can…"

His voice trailed off as Lucas turned and opened a bottom drawer on his desk. Flipping through a number of file folders, he finally settled on one and began thumbing through its contents. He extracted a single piece of paper and handed it over to Gideon.

"That's my copy," he said. "But you can keep it. I can always get another."

Ignoring the question of why Richards wouldn't have brought this up at their first meeting, Gideon scanned the report, his frown deepening with every word.

"This says he was spotted with a girl." He leveled an accusatory glare at Lucas. "You never mentioned a girl."

Lucas grimaced. "Because she's not important. Toby insisted she was his girlfriend, but I've never been able to get any information on her, other than her first name. It's like she doesn't exist."

"I'll assume that means she wasn't questioned about the murder."

"Did you miss the part where I don't even know her last name? And she took off before the police caught her. All I know about the girl is that Toby was spending a lot of money on her, and that they were always going to some new club called Sangre. I couldn't even find *that*, let alone Tricia. Which is why I brought you in."

Though he didn't let it show, everything inside Gideon froze.

Sangre.

That wasn't a new club. And there was a reason Lucas Richards couldn't find it. Nobody knew about Sangre except vampires and their human playthings. And since Toby wasn't a vampire, that left only one other possible permutation.

Maybe Toby wasn't the one who'd been affected by whatever was in the warehouse. Maybe it was the mysterious girl. Considering what Gideon had done to Jesse—someone he had a long, trusting history with—it was more than feasible that someone with less of an emotional investment would go too far.

"You should've told me about all this from the start," Gideon said. He rose from the corner of the desk and headed for the door. "Next time you want a job done right, don't start by cutting it off at the knees."

"Does it mean something?" When Gideon didn't stop, Lucas bolted from his chair and darted forward to stand between him and the door. "If you've found something out, tell me. This is my son we're talking about."

"No." It was pointless to get the man filled with false hope. "I haven't. But I will." He brushed past Lucas, blocking out the specter of guilt that he'd seen in the man's eyes. "I'll be in touch."

Lucas didn't stop him this time, which was a relief. Gideon had enough on his mind, not to have to deal with someone else's fear. Something was going on at that warehouse, and he'd dragged Jess into the middle of it.

He had to find out what it was before the next victim was someone he cared about.

CHAPTER 4

Jesse handled the oddly ornate doorknob with care. It seemed far too elaborate to belong to the busted door at the warehouse, and yet, he had found it among the boards and slivers, like it was where it was always meant to be. There was some sort of greasy substance coating the bottom of it that he couldn't identify—but not for lack of trying. Was this the last object Gideon touched before he…

Jesse shivered. Just the thought of the week before sent chills down his spine. Gideon had been firm…Jesse grimaced. Bad choice of words. Gideon was strict about no touching, no contact, nothing that could be distracting or misconstrued.

But he couldn't shake the feeling—or rather the fervent hope—that whatever was on this misplaced knob would be the way to break down the very tall wall that was now between them.

As if summoned by his thoughts, Gideon sauntered into the kitchen. Jesse swallowed, holding up the small object. "Does this seem familiar to you?"

Gideon plucked it from his fingers, turning it over in his hands. A slow frown drew his brows together, and he held it up to his nose, taking a long sniff.

"This is from the warehouse," he said. "How'd you get it?"

"I went to the warehouse and found it, Gideon." He arched his brow. "You know, as part of the investigation we're ostensibly conducting." Which was a lie, but he didn't think Gideon would call him a liar to his face.

27

Gideon's frown deepened. "I thought we agreed you were going to stay away from there."

"I don't think I agreed to that," Jesse countered mildly. "We're looking for something that causes a powerful reaction in demons that make them uncontrollable. Wouldn't it be a good idea to actually check out the scene of a…well…an incident?"

"It would be if you hadn't nearly died the last time." Gideon set the knob down on the table, and as it tilted back and forth in a short arc, he brought his fingers back to his nose. "Why does this smell funny?"

Jess glanced up. "I don't know."

"You don't smell it?"

"No. I don't have super-senses, remember?"

"Well, have you analyzed it?" Gideon didn't wait for a response. He rubbed his fingers against his thumb, as if testing the texture. "Huh. It felt like there was a lot more a second ago."

"I've tried to analyze it," Jesse said, watching Gideon carefully. The hair on the back of his neck was on end, and he felt a little warm. "I don't have all the necessary equipment for a full analysis right now."

Gideon seemed intent on his fingertips, their movement slowing. By the time they stopped, the greasy substance that had transferred from the door knob was gone.

He didn't lift his head. Instead, Gideon looked at Jess through his lashes. A shiver ran down Jesse's spine.

"You're wearing rubber gloves," he commented, almost too casually. "I'm going to bet it's not because you were hoping to check my prostate. Because we both know you wouldn't bother covering up for that."

It was the slight darkening of his tone that made Jesse's stomach clench. "I thought it would be smart to wear protective gear before handling strange items."

"But you handed it to me without hesitation." Slowly, Gideon shook his head, clicking his tongue in reproof. "Do you think I'm dumb, Jess? Did you think I wouldn't figure it out?"

"I don't think you're dumb, but I didn't know…"

Being around Gideon all the time had a tendency to make Jess forget how fast he could be. Before the last word was out of his mouth, the table was pushed screeching out of the way and Gideon's hand was at his throat. He didn't squeeze, but merely held him firm, pulling with enough strength to force Jess to rise to his feet if he didn't want to lose his head.

"I hate it when you lie to me," Gideon said. He pushed Jess back against the wall, but continued moving until their bodies were flush. "Too bad I thought you'd actually learned something the last time we were in this position."

Jesse's hands hung uselessly at his side. It wouldn't do any good to try to push Gideon away. He tried to swallow, but Gideon's grip was tight enough to prevent that, though he wasn't blocking his air. "I did."

"Oh? And what did you learn? It wasn't how not to piss off a vampire, that's for sure."

He felt more than a hint of fear now. Gideon's face was inscrutable. He hadn't been angry like this before, and if there was anything beneath the rage, Jesse didn't see it. "I'm sorry, Gideon."

Though Gideon didn't loosen his grip, Jess felt his fingertips begin to massage the sides of his neck.

"Do you even know what you're sorry for, Jess?" His voice was lower, almost silken, and it made Jesse's heart speed up even more. "Because I don't believe for a second you are. I think you deliberately put yourself in danger in order to satisfy some urge to get under my skin again. I don't think you regret any of it."

It was hard to imagine regretting any action that put Gideon's body against his, any decision that finally made Gideon touch him again. He understood why Gideon thought he needed to keep his distance, he did, but he didn't think Gideon understood how much Jess needed this. "You're right."

The admission softened the glint in Gideon's eyes, though his jaw remained firm. "You're lucky desperation makes you smell like fucking nirvana," he said. "But if you think you're going to get anywhere near my cock with this little stunt, think again." He leaned in, pressing his mouth to Jesse's ear. "Bad boys don't deserve to be rewarded when they're naughty, now do they, Jess?"

Jesse tensed, imagining Gideon's tongue against his skin, the scrape of his teeth. It was a good thing the question had only one logical answer, because he was very distracted. "No...no they don't."

"I'm glad we're in agreement, then."

Suddenly, they were moving, and Jess stumbled along after Gideon, his wrists suddenly trapped in one of Gideon's powerful hands. Gideon pulled him from the kitchen, not looking back, and headed straight for the stairs, up the single flight and through the deserted office to the spare room.

Jesse's stomach seized. Only one thing happened in that room, and usually Gideon kicked him out when it happened. For whatever reasons, he didn't like Jesse to witness his interrogations. He'd been in it when Gideon wasn't around, of course. And he knew what he would find this time.

The room was dark, but Gideon navigated with ease, pulling Jess to the opposite wall to stand before a glass-fronted cabinet. Without letting go of his wrists, Gideon opened a door and reached in to extract a pair of thick manacles.

Jesse licked his lips nervously, eyeing the manacles. "But they're punished?" he asked, unable to quell the part of him that wanted to have all the right answers.

In the dim light, Gideon's eyes seemed to glow. "You call it punishment. I call it happy hour."

The manacles snapped around Jesse's wrists, heavy and cold. He didn't have time to assess their weight before Gideon stepped to the middle of the room and lifted them over his head. The chains linking them looped perfectly over a hook that hung from the ceiling, pulling the muscles in Jesse's sides as he stretched, and Gideon closed the metal tab that locked the hook shut.

There would be no escaping. It didn't matter. He didn't want to go anywhere anyway.

Jesse trembled. Now that he was utterly at Gideon's mercy, he shook with delight, with anticipation. His clothes felt more restricting than the manacles, and he felt bereft without any contact at all. He couldn't predict Gideon, couldn't second guess him, and though he had read everything there was to read about what he'd been like before he'd changed his existence around to fight for good, there was no literature to guide him in this situation. Gideon—his friend—was an unknown, and that, somehow, excited Jess more than anything else.

Gideon walked past him to flip the light switch, then went back to the cabinet. A low sound filled the room, and it took a moment for Jess to realize what it was. Gideon was *humming*. Like he was in a good mood. Like he was looking forward to what was about to happen.

Jesse's cock jumped. Gideon could deny it all he wanted, but if he really didn't want anything to do with Jess, he would've left well enough alone back in the kitchen. The substance on the door knob had simply erased any inhibitions Gideon might have had about holding back.

He watched with a pounding heart as Gideon picked up first one thing and then another. With his back turned, it was impossible to see for sure what Gideon was doing, but that dialed up the anticipation even further.

"You didn't like those clothes, right?" Gideon finally commented.

"No," Jesse said quickly. He didn't care about the clothes at all. He'd buy more, later. He'd never wear clothes again, if that's what Gideon wanted.

"Good. They're in the way."

A knife suddenly appeared in his hand, and he sauntered toward Jesse with long, lazy steps. Jess held his breath as Gideon began slicing off the buttons on his shirt, one by one from the bottom, and when it hung open, Gideon ran the flat of the blade down the middle of Jesse's chest.

The knife was cold on his skin, and Jesse sucked his breath in and tried to arch away from the blade. Gideon put the flat of his hand against Jesse's back, forcing him against the knife again. Jesse nearly whimpered. If nothing else, being with Gideon reminded him of how vulnerable he was.

"What? This wasn't what you wanted? Now how did I possibly misgauge that?"

The knife whispered through Jesse's clothes, shredding the fabric so that it fell effortlessly to the floor. Not once did Jess feel the blade against his skin again, but all too soon, Gideon was stepping away, leaving him naked and hard with anticipation.

His throat went dry when Gideon pulled his own shirt off, revealing his tightly sculpted back. "Good to know I didn't misgauge this getting you hot, though," Gideon commented. "What exactly do you think is going to happen here, Jess?"

Jesse felt the undeniable urge to apologize for being wary of the knife. "I don't know," he murmured, and he felt like apologizing for that as well. "Please tell me."

"A lesson." He turned back, and from his hand dangled a cat o'nine tails. "Maybe when we're done here, you'll remember to be a little more straight up with me. Honesty will get you a hell of a lot farther than fucking with me, Jess."

"I *was* honest with you," Jesse protested. He twisted in the chains, his eye on the whip. "I was honest with you, and it didn't get me anywhere."

Gideon prowled around the edge of the room, and though he struggled to follow him, Jess soon lost sight of where he was.

"You gave me the door knob, knowing it was tainted," Gideon said.

Whether he was deliberately ignoring Jesse's meaning, he had no idea. He simply wished he could see what Gideon was doing. "You did it deliberately to see what would happen."

There wasn't time for a response. The crack of leather split the air.

Jesse trapped the howl in his throat, and his lungs seized, the sudden contact freezing the air in his chest. He was more shocked than hurt, but the shock enveloped him completely. His cock jerked, a single thread of pleasure winding its way down his spine and to his groin.

"I'm sorry," Jesse gasped, when he could speak. "It won't happen again."

Gideon chuckled. "You're lying. You've got balls, I'll give you that. But if you thought it would get you what you wanted, you'd do it again." The whip cracked again. Slivers of heat sliced down Jesse's back. "Admit it."

It occurred to him to lie again, but he suspected Gideon's reaction would be the same whether he told the truth or not. "I would if I thought we'd both get what we wanted."

"And what's that?"

"You don't want to have to care about the consequences." The whip landed across his shoulders. "You want to be the one in charge." And lower on his ribs. "You think you should be able to do whatever you want to me, and, God, Gideon, I want that, too." The whip whistled through the air behind him, erupting like fire across his skin. Jesse cried out, unable to ignore the pain any longer.

So wrapped in the searing agony now making his skin throb, he never heard Gideon move.

"I *should* be able to do whatever I want to you," Gideon murmured in Jesse's ear. His bare chest pressed to Jess' back, and the cool contact helped ease some of the sting. "But right now, I'll settle for this."

The first touch of Gideon's tongue along his split skin made Jess cry out again, but this time, it was a sound of shocked pleasure.

Jesse writhed against Gideon's mouth, but never attempted to pull away from him. If anything, he wanted more contact. Gideon abandoned his broken skin and sought out the long thin lines of blood rolling down his back. Each swipe of Gideon's tongue soothed every sliver of pain, until he was quivering with pleasure and need, the sting from the whip almost entirely forgotten.

"I smell you everywhere." Gideon's voice floated up to him, caressing hands gliding around the front of his thighs. "In the office, in my bed. Do you know I can't bring myself to change my sheets ever since you spent the day in them? You need to bleed more often. I don't think my cock's been soft since I fucked you."

Jesse moaned. He knew Gideon wanted him, but remembering a long night of fucking was not the same as hearing the words come from Gideon's mouth. Gideon moved his hands over his thighs, his fingers framing Jesse's stiff cock without actually touching him. He wanted Gideon to make him bleed, wanted Gideon to fuck him, wanted Gideon to touch him, wanted Gideon to bite him...

Rivulets of blood trickled down his back, disappearing one by one. Gideon's tongue traced over swells of flesh until Jess felt his mouth at the upper curve of his ass. His heart thumped, and he stood a little straighter, spreading his legs on instinct in order to open himself up.

"I already said you weren't going to be rewarded," Gideon chastised. He came around Jesse's body, standing tall and pressing his blood-slick chest to Jess'. "You don't get my cock, and I'm not touching your ass." He smirked. "Not even if you beg."

Jesse leaned forward, stretching his neck to tentatively lick the patch of skin beneath Gideon's jaw. For a moment, he savored the taste of Gideon's skin—which led him to thoughts of other areas of Gideon he wanted to taste. "I don't get your cock at all?"

"No." His eyes turned golden. "I get yours."

Blood smeared down Jesse's body as Gideon slid down. His breath caught in his throat as Gideon grasped his cock at the root, angling it away from his body. With one last wicked leer, Gideon dropped his jaw and swallowed Jess down in one stroke.

Jesse fought the temptation to close his eyes—he needed to watch Gideon. He tensed, expecting to feel razor sharp fangs against his shaft, but Gideon was surprisingly careful. He pulled back, sliding his warm mouth along Jesse's shaft, and then swallowed him once more, his teeth barely scraping against his cock. Gideon looked up, his golden eyes sending a shockwave through Jesse's body.

"Oh..." Jesse panted. "Oh...Gideon...I'm..."

He was trying to warn Gideon, desperate not to let this end, but Gideon created hard suction around his shaft, and Jesse exploded deep in his throat, his cock jerking several times against Gideon's rough tongue.

The manacles rattled from how hard Jess was shaking, but Gideon didn't move off his cock even when he'd stopped coming. Instead, he sucked at it, slipping his tongue into the slit to chase stray droplets. Only when Jesse started softening did he pull off.

Gideon stood and stepped back, putting several inches between them. If he tried, Jess imagined he might be able to push himself enough to gain contact, but his muscles failed him, and he only watched as Gideon undid his pants.

"My turn," he said simply.

Fresh hope burned in Jesse's gut, but Gideon didn't advance. He stood there, eyes heavy on Jess, and fisted his cock, stroking it in long, hard pulls from tip to root.

Watching Gideon made Jesse forget he had already come. His pale skin was still streaked with blood, and his hard cock was glistening, and Jesse knew what that little drop would taste like. He was still waiting to taste all of Gideon's come, and he couldn't believe that Gideon truly intended to deny them both. But Gideon didn't take a step forward, just watched Jesse watch him.

"Gideon...please..." He knew Gideon said begging wouldn't do any good, but he thought it was worth a shot.

His hand moved a little bit faster. "Say it again."

Hope ignited in his chest, his balls ached, and his ass clenched. "Please, Gideon. Fuck me. Fuck my mouth. Need to feel you. Please."

A sound that was half-grunt, half-groan, came from Gideon's throat. "You do look pretty when you beg," he murmured. He took a step forward. "You look prettier painted in my spunk."

There were precious seconds where Gideon's hand was a near blur, where Jesse couldn't breathe for that fragile hope still choking him, where all he could see was the muscles working in Gideon's upper body. Gideon's head dropped back, the sinew of his neck standing out, and with a feral cry, he stripped his cock one last time before he exploded, his come crossing the distance to land on Jesse's stomach, in the coarse hair at the base of his cock, everywhere Jesse couldn't reach.

Jesse looked down, watching the thick fluid roll down his skin with sharp disappointment. His wrists felt raw from the manacles, and he ached from his neck to his ass, and still, all he thought about was how much he had wanted Gideon's cock. At that point, he would be happy with Gideon's teeth. He needed that connection. It didn't even feel like a sexual need anymore. It felt more basic, like a thirst that settled in the back of his throat.

And Gideon knew it.

Averting his eyes, because the sight of Gideon's body was making it worse, he muttered, "I think my fingers are numb."

Without tucking away his cock, Gideon grabbed a set of keys from the cupboard. The hard length pressed into Jesse's side when Gideon stretched to unlock the manacles, smearing the come around. It was a terrible tease. He didn't need to see Gideon's eyes to know it was deliberate.

The moment the pressure was relieved on his burning muscles, Jesse sagged, wondering how he'd be able to stand. The strong band of Gideon's arm came around his back to support him, and he looked up to meet his eyes.

"Have you learned your lesson?" Gideon asked. All frivolity was gone.

Jesse had learned his lesson, and for a moment, he despaired. Gideon would not seek out the substance that acted as a catalyst for both encounters, and Jesse didn't think anything had changed for Gideon, either. But he couldn't imagine coming to work every day, being near Gideon, talking to him, touching him, watching him, and being content to remain friends, as if nothing had ever happened at all. There had to be a way around both unwanted options.

"I have," Jesse said softly. "I shouldn't have tried to trick you. It won't happen again."

"Good."

Without another word, Gideon led him from the room, half-carrying him back down the stairs when his legs failed to work properly. He dropped him unceremoniously on the couch and retreated before Jess could touch him further.

"I'm going out," he said. "Do what you have to in order to clean yourself up."

Jesse nodded, wondering if Gideon realized this sort of treatment hurt him far more than getting fucked in an alley, or chained to the ceiling. He only hoped that when Gideon came back to himself, there wouldn't be another round of apologies—for either of them. Though the chances of that were slim to none.

Gideon walked out of the apartment without another word, but Jesse didn't feel like he had the energy to make it to the bathroom. He went as far as the kitchen to find a towel and wiped his chest clean before stumbling back to collapse on the couch. Careful not to aggravate his back, he curled up on the oversized sofa and tried to figure out what was to be done.

·

CHAPTER 5

The entire time Gideon cooked breakfast, he heard Jesse's even breathing coming from the living room. He had returned from his night out right before dawn to find Jess asleep on the couch, and all he had felt was guilt. He'd been angry at the trick, and he'd acted without thought, without care that this was his best friend he was toying with. As Jesse had known he would. As Jesse had hoped he would, though Gideon suspected he'd envisioned an encounter a little less bloody.

He wanted to carry Jess into the bedroom and let him sleep it out in there, but the scent of his blood still hung thick in the air and pretty bruises had blossomed along his friend's skin, colors that made Gideon want to lick and nibble flesh he shouldn't touch. Leaving him on the couch was safer, if not as comfortable. So he was making it up to him by fixing breakfast.

Not that some scrambled eggs and bacon said *I'm sorry for flaying you* very well. But it was a start. And after they were done eating, Gideon was going to have a long talk to Jesse about what exactly he thought he was doing.

He set the table, but before going to wake Jess, he fetched a loose T-shirt and sweats for him to wear. He was going to have to start including a wardrobe allowance in their budgeting if he kept this up.

When he walked into the living room, Gideon paused. Jess was awake.

"I brought you some clothes," he said, awkwardly thrusting them out. "And there's eggs. And bacon."

Jesse studied him warily for a moment before nodding accepting the clothes. He moved a little stiffly as he dressed, but ⟶ didn't make a sound, or even wince in pain. He silently made his way to the kitchen, detouring to the cabinet where Gideon kept his painkillers and helping himself to several, before sitting at the table.

"It smells good."

It was both easier and more difficult to face Jesse when he was this calm. While Gideon wasn't eager to think Jess was in pain, the fact that he refused to even show it had to mean he was more hurt by what happened than he was willing to admit to Gideon. He carried over the hot mugs—coffee for Jess, blood for himself—and sat down opposite him. Waiting to talk was a bad idea.

"What did you think you were doing?" Gideon winced inwardly. The question came out angrier than he'd hoped. He supposed he still harbored some feelings about being manipulated.

Jesse took a long sip from his coffee before answering. "If it makes you feel better to think it was all my fault, that's fine. But I didn't thrust the knob into your hand. You took it from me, without, I might add, noticing the gloves I wore. I didn't force anything on you. But you know what? It doesn't really make a difference. Because I'm tired of both of us trying to pretend that everything is normal."

Gideon frowned. "What are you talking about? Everything *will* be normal again, if we keep that stuff—whatever it is—away from me."

Jesse looked at him with a combination of exasperation and amusement. "No, Gideon, it's not. It won't be. I was happy before to pretend that I didn't want you, and you didn't know it. But I can't now. And you sure as hell can't pretend you don't know what I…want from you."

The echoes of his pleading filled Gideon's ears, and he fought not to squirm in his seat as his cock hardened. "What about what I want?" he countered. "You're the best friend and partner I've ever had. Doesn't that count for anything?"

"What makes you think I'd stop being those things, Gideon? I'm still your friend. I still know you better than anybody, and the only way I'd ever stop being your partner is if you fired me. And we both know you'd never do that, because you don't like to research."

"Because sex is messy, Jess. Especially the kind of sex…" He braced himself for being honest. "…I'd want."

"That's why we shower afterward," Jess joked, but it fell flat. "Gideon, the kind of sex you want is the kind of sex I want. You

me, or horrified me, or maimed me, or damaged me.
ting adults, and I'm not so naïve I don't know what

at the mug of blood he cradled between his broad
ell me that given the choice, you wouldn't want the
candlelight and roses route, Jess. Hell, that's what you deserve. Not being treated like a toy for me to drag out whenever I feel the urge."

"First, I do not have an unfulfilled need for candlelight and roses. And even if I did, messy sex doesn't preclude those things. Secondly, Gideon, what do I have to do to convince you that I want to be dragged out whenever you feel the urge? I don't want to be treated like a toy, true, but I do want to be treated like *your* toy."

Lifting his head, Gideon met Jesse's earnest gaze, noting the slight lean in the other man's upper body as he angled himself closer. It was the way he always was, Gideon realized now. Always trying to fill the space around Gideon, always there filling his senses. It was as much who he was as the fact that Gideon noticed. Jesse had preoccupied his thoughts more than once since coming into his life.

Was it so bad, what he was suggesting? Jess was right; he wanted it or, at least, he thought he wanted it. And Gideon craved the freedom to touch Jess the way he dreamed about, without fear of recrimination. The drawback rested in the possibility of dissension later on. Gideon had enough exes he'd been forced to walk away from. He didn't want to add Jesse to that list.

He leaned back in his chair, sprawling his legs out in front of him. It gave Jess a clear view of the bulge in Gideon's crotch, though at the moment, Jess seemed too intent on his face to notice.

"All right," Gideon said. "Convince me."

Jesse blinked, straightening like Gideon had slapped him. He only hesitated for a moment before sliding off the chair and onto his knees between Gideon's thighs. There was a distinctively hungry gleam in Jess' eyes, reminding Gideon of all the pleading from the day before. Keeping his eyes locked on Gideon's face, he unzipped Gideon's pants and wrapped his fingers around his erection.

Though the contact made him want to sigh in satisfaction, Gideon remained stoic, refusing to even unfold his arms to reach out to Jess. "I have certain expectations of my partners," he said. "And I'm still a vampire, remember. I bite, I like to hurt, and I love to make people bleed."

"I'll start taking iron supplements so I won't become anemic," Jesse answered, calmly.

"I've never found a boundary I didn't rip out of my way. If you're not prepared to follow me, this thing between us doesn't even get off the ground."

"I always thought it was a given that I'd follow you wherever you wanted to go."

Gideon finally reached out and rested a hand on the top of Jesse's head. "You haven't seen a fraction of the places I go," he warned. He began pushing Jess toward his hips, but instead of aiming him for his cock, he pushed him lower until his nose was nuzzling Gideon's balls.

"Show me," Jesse murmured, before drawing his tongue along Gideon's skin, first tracing one ball, then the other. He used his tongue, teeth, and lips without hesitation, lapping and sucking eagerly.

It was hard not to groan at the dark promise in Jesse's tone. It had been a long time since Gideon had found anybody as willing as Jess, and the lengths he actually believed Jess would go made him want to shoot on the spot. When he was touching Gideon like this, it was hard to remember his rationalization for not pursuing it earlier.

But Jesse's offer suggested something else to Gideon. It was possible to show Jess how different their worlds really were, that he didn't want Gideon completely unleashed. It was simply a matter of pushing him through the wrong door.

Knotting his fingers in Jesse's hair, Gideon pulled him off his balls, smiling slightly at the disappointment gleaming in Jesse's eyes. "I think that's an excellent idea," he said. "We'll make it a date. One week from tonight."

"One week." He looked down at Gideon's cock. "Are we going to do anything else between then and now?"

"We?" Gideon shook his head. "You, on the other hand, had better get to sucking me off. And remember it's going to have to last you for a week."

That, apparently, was all the encouragement Jesse needed. He experimentally slid the tip of his tongue from the base to the tip of Gideon's cock, before wrapping his lips around the head. As he sucked on the sensitive flesh, his tongue dipped into the slit, teasing out drops of pre-come.

Gideon kept his hand loose on the top of Jesse's head, ready to start setting the pace if Jess continued to toy with him too much. "There are things you're going to do this week in preparation for our night out," he said. His gaze was fixed on the contrast of Jesse's mouth against his cock, the tight suction of the red lips as he continued to savor Gideon's pre-come. Fuck, but Jess had a gorgeous mouth. It was going to be a real treat to see it put to good use finally. "The first of which is, you will not come in that time period. I want you primed for what I have in mind."

Jesse looked up at him through his lashes, his assent bright and clear in his eyes. He moved his mouth down Gideon's shaft, swallowing more and more of his length, but still moving slowly, as if trying to prolong the entire experience. Gideon sighed as the tip of his cock finally brushed against the back of Jess' throat. His tongue was still busy, snaking around his shaft.

"Second..." The temptation to lean back and close his eyes to appreciate this was great, but Gideon knew he had to say what needed to be said. "You're going to shave. I want your balls smooth as silk when I suck on them."

Jesse grunted, cupping Gideon's balls while he pulled back. Jess massaged his sac lightly as he began to move his head. It seemed like he was swallowing his cock farther each time Jess slid forward. Like the time in the alley, Jess didn't seem to hold anything back.

Gideon slid lower in the seat, widening his legs to encourage Jesse's exploration. With a subtle pressure, he began to push on the other man's head and this time, when the tip of his cock hit the back of Jesse's throat, Gideon didn't let up. He kept on pushing until he felt the tight muscles constrict around his length and Jesse's lips buried into his crotch.

"And, third, leave your ass alone." He held Jess in place, waiting until those lashes lifted and they were looking into each other's eyes. "You're going to be tempted to get yourself ready, maybe stretch yourself out so that you don't have to wait so long. Don't. I want you as tight as possible for me." Gideon grinned. "And really, you're going to stretch around me soon enough. Let's make it a little more fun."

Jesse moaned, the vibrations going through Gideon's cock and straight to his balls. When Gideon loosened his grip on the back of Jess' head, Jess didn't take his eyes from Gideon's as he pulled all the way back, almost letting his cock fall from his lips. Gideon increased the pressure on Jesse's skull, slamming him back down. He moved without resistance, his teeth barely scraping the length of his shaft, and once again, Jess' throat constricted around the tip.

Gideon lifted his other hand to Jesse's head, taking him between both hands in order to hold him properly. He fucked Jesse's mouth in bruising strokes, each one harder than the last, and all the while, Jess kept the suction around his shaft tight, taking him in and letting him out with intense eyes locked on Gideon's. Too soon, Gideon's balls tightened, and the fire in his belly coiled, and in a single stroke, he buried his cock in Jesse's throat, shooting deep as Jess swallowed every drop.

Only when his cock stopped twitching did Gideon let go of Jesse's head. "Stand up," he ordered.

Jesse stood, but not before sliding his tongue over Gideon's shaft one more time. The sweats outlined Jess' erection, and he shifted his weight from one foot to the other. He was breathing a bit faster than normal, and Gideon heard his heart hammer. He didn't have to say a word to betray how aroused he was. Gideon saw the pain of it in his eyes.

Reaching forward, Gideon pushed down the elastic waistband with one hand and freed Jesse's cock with the other. He used his hold to tug Jess closer, but stopped shy of his mouth, inhaling the musky scent of his skin.

"God, you smell good," Gideon murmured. Slowly, he began pumping Jesse's length. "Almost as good as you taste."

Jesse put a bracing hand on Gideon's shoulder, his fingers digging into Gideon's flesh as he compulsively gripped and relaxed his hold. Jess whimpered on the down strokes, almost as if Gideon was pulling the strangled sound from his throat with each jerk of his wrist.

Jess wouldn't last long; of that, Gideon was certain. With a wicked grin, he reached between Jesse's legs, tracing a path across his balls to the soft skin behind them, all the way to his tight hole. Jess moaned and spread his legs farther. Gideon almost laughed. Like he needed the invitation to his ass anyway. Deliberately, he pressed two fingers deep into his passage.

"Oh...Gideon..." He gasped, his back arching. When his fingers brushed against Jess' prostate, he tensed, his ass clenching around Gideon's hand. That was the sign he was waiting for. He tightened his grip, squeezing Jesse's cock harder and jerking his wrist forward. "Gideon."

Jesse exploded in Gideon's waiting mouth, his hot come splashing against his tongue, a few strings clinging to his lips. Gideon held him there until Jesse's cock stopped trembling in his hand.

Without letting him go, Gideon slid gracefully to his feet, pressing their bodies together as he slammed his mouth to Jesse's. Jess parted

41

immediately, and Gideon thrust his tongue inside, sharing the sticky fluid. The kiss was greedy and loud, though Jesse's moans were louder, and Gideon folded his free arm around Jess' back, molding himself around the other man.

Jess' hands snuck up Gideon's back to grip his shirt. He clung to him like he didn't plan to let anything separate them. Heat seeped from his skin and into Gideon's, and his willingness, his eagerness, was communicated through every inch of his tense, damp body. Gideon deepened the kiss, pushing what was left of the come over Jesse's tongue. He felt the muscles in Jesse's jaw and throat work as he swallowed.

It occurred to Gideon when they finally parted and Jess was leaning his sweaty brow against Gideon's cheek, that it was their first real kiss. There had been plenty of caresses that night in the alley and afterward, but that had been under the effect of whatever poison was in the warehouse. Those didn't count. This…this long, hungry, sensual exploration was the real deal.

He grazed his lips over Jesse's cheek, closing his eyes as he got lost in the hot breath on his neck and the vibrations still pulsing through Jesse's body. Maybe his fears that pushing their relationship to a new level would spoil their friendship were silly. He cared about Jess as much as he wanted him, and if that kiss was any indication of what was to come…

Gideon stopped the thoughts before they took root too deeply.

Time would tell. The true test would be in a week. Only then could he dare to hope that Jess would fit into a life they both wanted.

<u>CHAPTER 6</u>

Jesse's excitement for the date didn't fade, even as his apprehension grew. He wasn't nervous about whatever Gideon had planned—though he was painfully curious—but he couldn't stop thinking about what it meant. He didn't have to be told it was a test, and if he failed, that would be the end of whatever it was they had.

He felt he'd passed the first part of the test. It was difficult to avoid touching himself; it felt like he was constantly aroused. A single glance from Gideon made him hard, and any contact—no matter how incidental—made him ache. But Gideon was all business, and Jess had to constantly remind himself that they had *work* to do, a *case* to solve, and he couldn't spend hours and hours thinking about Gideon.

Well, he could, and he did, but he *shouldn't*.

Jess couldn't even believe he was in the situation to begin with. No matter how much he'd hoped, no matter how much he privately fantasized, he never thought it would actually happen. He knew Gideon didn't love him—not like he loved Gideon—but it didn't really matter. Gideon valued him, and respected him, and above all, *wanted* him. How had that happened? When had that happened?

The morning of the Big Date—which had already reached nearly epic status in Jesse's mind—Gideon wasn't in the office. Or his apartment. But he did leave something behind for Jess to find. A midnight blue silk shirt and a pair of black pants waited for him on the kitchen table. Beside them was a new pair of shoes. On top of the shirt rested a thick black collar, clearly designed for a human neck, and a short leather leash, next to a cock ring. There was no note, but Jesse didn't need it.

He ignored the gifts throughout the day. Or tried to. He tried to focus on his research, but he was counting down the minutes and quickly realizing it was going to be the longest day of his life. He listened for Gideon's return, but he was left alone for the entire day, with nothing but his thoughts, his books, and his hard-on. Finally, before sunset, Jesse abandoned his research in favor of his new clothes.

Jesse began with the cock ring, wincing slightly as he slid it down his shaft. It was going to be a long, long night. The shirt fit perfectly, as did the pants, as though Gideon had had them tailor-made. Jesse closed the collar around his neck last, admiring himself in the bathroom mirror.

"You look good enough to eat."

He jumped at the sound of Gideon's voice, whirling to see him lounging against the jamb of the open bathroom door. The remark about vampires without reflections sneaking up on unsuspecting humans died long before it reached his tongue, however. He could only stare as he drank in Gideon's appearance.

A black cashmere sweater stretched over his broad shoulders, hugging where it tapered down his muscled body. It was paired with leather pants Jess had only seen him wear when they'd had to go out undercover, but they molded over his hips like a second skin, revealing the definite bulge of his arousal. In his hands dangled the leash Jess had left lying in the other room, the thin leather strap gliding through his fingers as he toyed with it.

"I figure since I ruined so many of your other clothes, the least I could do was get you some new ones," Gideon said. "Are they all right?"

"They're great." He ran his hands down his chest, smoothing the shirt over his skin. It was probably one of the finest things Jess had ever worn. "Thank you." His fingers itched to run over Gideon's sweater, to feel the ripple of his muscled chest beneath his hand. He couldn't deny himself the contact and his fingers drifted from Gideon's shoulder to his waist. "You look pretty good yourself."

Gideon's grin was wolfish. "Good enough to eat, I hope."

"Yes, absolutely," Jesse murmured, pressing his body against Gideon's.

Gideon ran his hand up Jesse's arm, the leather leash snaking along behind to send a cascade of shivers down Jesse's spine. His gaze flickered from Jesse's to the collar, and then lower for a fraction of a second. "From the scent of you, I know you followed at least one of my instructions." His eyes were black with desire when he lifted them again. "What about the others?"

Jesse swallowed. "To the letter."

Shaving had been ridiculously difficult. First, wielding a sharp razor blade in the vicinity of his balls made him nervous—what if he nicked himself? Second, every time he thought why he was shaving, his cock jerked, increasing the chances of nicking himself considerably. It would have been infinitely easier without the erection, but he didn't want to violate the first instruction in order to achieve the second.

"Though it wasn't easy."

The clear whisk of metal as Gideon snapped the leash into place made Jesse's chest hitch, but he kept still as the hand that had held it now slid down his chest, not stopping until it reached the waistband he'd only just finished closing.

"I should probably check to be sure," Gideon murmured.

His deft fingers undid the button and zipper, cool against Jesse's heated shaft when they reached inside. Jess gasped when Gideon reached down to cup his sac, stroking the smooth skin, and his eyes fluttered shut when a rumble of approval came from Gideon's chest.

"This has been the longest week of my life," Jesse admitted. "And it didn't help not knowing what you had planned," he added, looking to Gideon hopefully.

He appeared thoughtful as he traced the cock ring with a single fingertip. "I didn't realize you needed schedules for dates, too," he teased.

"No, I suppose I don't *need* a schedule," Jesse said, striving to keep his voice normal, even though the simple touch was making his head spin. "It would be nice, is all."

"Oh, it's going to be better than nice. The club we're going to is one of my favorites."

"Club?" Gideon didn't like people, and he didn't like buying overpriced, watered-down drinks, and he didn't like loud music, and he especially didn't like dancing. Jesse suddenly became certain that Gideon's favorite club was one that he had never visited before, and probably one that he wouldn't want to visit alone.

Gideon's gaze was unwavering. "A vampire club. Called Sangre." He paused, and his hand stilled. "This is your last chance to back out, Jess. Humans don't go to Sangre unless they're escorted by vampires.

And they only go for pretty much one reason. Once you're inside, there's no turning around."

Everything from his groin to his throat clenched. He was on the brink now, and if he had the courage to jump, Gideon would be waiting for him at the bottom of the fall. Or he could back away, go back to the relative safety of watching the vampire from afar. Gideon waited patiently while Jess turned both options over in his mind, but ultimately, there was only one option truly worth considering.

"I'm not going to back out."

Gideon removed his hand from Jesse's pants, reaching up to grip the back of his neck. He pulled Jess closer until their mouths were faintly touching and murmured, "Just remember. You're there with me. Whatever else happens, I'm never going to let anybody hurt you, Jess."

Jesse inclined his head slightly. "I know." His trust in Gideon was implicit, a solid, unmovable object in his life. "I've always known that."

Gideon's lips parted, and he tugged Jess the rest of the way in order to capture his mouth in a slow, lazy kiss. His leather pants scraped across Jesse's exposed cock, making him ache for even more contact, but for now, Jess was content to savor the kiss he'd wanted all week long.

"We better go," Gideon said when they finally parted. His voice was rough, and his fingers caressed Jesse's nape as he dragged them away. "Otherwise, I'm going to tie you to my bed and this whole plan will be ruined."

Jesse didn't have any problems with a plan that included tying him to the bed, but he didn't voice a protest as Gideon led him out of the bathroom. He tucked himself back in his pants quickly as they walked. He was zipped up by the time they reached the door, but Gideon didn't seem interested in releasing the leather rope.

"Are you going to hold onto that all the way to the club?"

The glance Gideon shot back at him was inscrutable, his eyes so fathomless that they arrested Jess in his spot. "You're mine," he said simply. As if that was all the explanation Jess needed.

Jesse nodded, hoping his face didn't reveal the swift flood of bliss through his body. He *was* Gideon's. He never had the courage to state it, and now he didn't need to. Gideon's announcement and his silent acquiescence was all that needed to be said.

As he followed Gideon to the car, he almost forgot entirely about the leash. What did that matter in the face of the fact they were going to a vampire club? He wasn't having second thoughts, but what he had agreed to was finally sinking in.

The ride was quiet but not uncomfortable. Gideon tuned the radio to something classical, and he hummed along as he navigated the dark streets. The leash remained loosely looped around his hand, and every time he turned a corner, it tugged a little at Jesse's neck, just enough to remind him that it was there. By the time Gideon pulled up to their destination, though, Jess was already accustomed to it.

A uniformed valet came around to Gideon's door, opening it for him to get out. "Stay in your seat," he murmured to Jess as he finally released the leather strap.

Jesse nodded, his eyes tracking Gideon as the other man walked around the front of the car. He glanced quickly at the front of the club, realizing he had walked past the building several times and never noticed it. It was entirely inconspicuous. How many times had Gideon visited it? What did he do while he was there? Jess didn't think he'd get a chance to ask during this trip, but he stored the question away for later.

Gideon opened the passenger door, but Jesse still didn't move.

The night masked Gideon's features from study, but his voice when he spoke was soft. "Out, boy."

Jesse's heart thudded. This was it. If he obeyed this order, he would have no choice but to obey them all. He stepped out of the car, stepping out of the way as the valet slammed the door behind him. The club still looked like an abandoned building, but he heard music now, and a certain energy radiated from the walls. Something intoxicating and frightening. Or maybe that was just Gideon.

In the darkness, Gideon found the end of the leash without fail. He turned on his heel and strode toward the front of the building, walking a pace ahead of Jess, and nodded at a large, black vampire seated by the door. The other vampire nodded back, rising from his stool to pull open the door. He never even gave Jesse a second look.

The first thing he noticed about the club's interior was the temperature. Most clubs Jess was familiar with were stifling, crowded places that left little room to breathe. Sangre was comfortably cool, in spite of the throngs of people that dotted the large, open room. Large fans overhead kept the air circulating, and the music that he'd detected outside made the atmosphere pulse. Not from a band, though. Huge speakers were scattered around the perimeter, filling the space with sound.

It might be full of vampires, but Sangre felt like a living creature. Jesse's heart sped up a little bit faster.

Gideon began leading him through the crowd, taking him past long, low couches populated with writhing bodies, and nooks where no light escaped, only the occasional cries and whispers. It took little time to realize vampires outnumbered humans by a ratio of almost ten to one, and even less to understand why he knew the difference. He wasn't the only one wearing a leash. At various points, groups of men and women were congregated around a single collared person, who was usually naked.

Jesse's mouth went dry. No wonder there was no band. The humans were Sangre's entertainment.

Gideon hadn't gone through any of the rules with him, or given him a single hint of what to expect. Was that part of the test? Jesse wasn't sure, but he thought it was best to err on the side of caution. He kept his mouth shut, and except for the occasional frantic glance around the club, he kept his eyes on the back of Gideon's neck. Despite his heightened senses, his excitement, his terror, and the growing ache in his groin, he couldn't help but notice how nice Gideon's shoulders were.

Gideon came to a stop at the bar, but Jess hung back as he ordered a pint of blood and a double whiskey. As they waited for the order to be filled, Gideon turned around and leaned against the bar, his elbows resting on the edge.

"So?" His gaze was glittering. It was difficult to tell in the dim lighting if that was a trick of Jesse's overactive imagination or a result of being so near to his demon. "What do you think?"

Jesse didn't respond immediately. *It's nice*, his typical non-answer, was entirely inappropriate. This place wasn't nice by any definition of the word. Scary? Loud? Thrilling? All true, but also probably not the answer Gideon wanted.

"It's not anything like I expected," Jesse said, not bothering to raise his voice over the music. He decided to go with honesty. If Gideon didn't want an honest response, he shouldn't have asked. "It's…a bit intimidating. But exciting. I've heard of places like this, of course, but I never thought I'd get a chance to see one from the inside." He smiled a little sheepishly. "That's not the only reason it's exciting, of course."

Gideon's lust-filled eyes raked over him, until Jess squirmed. "There aren't many rules here," he said. "Do as I say. Don't speak until spoken to." Their drinks arrived, and Gideon picked up the whiskey first and handed it to Jess. "That'll help you relax. I haven't seen you this tense since we got cornered by that mob down at the pier."

Jesse accepted the drink gladly. This would probably be much easier if he was a bit buzzed, though he didn't want to get drunk. He didn't want to have the temptation of blaming alcohol later for this. He needed to be fully aware of everything he did, everything he agreed to.

He downed it in one gulp, closing his eyes as the artificial fire spread through his veins. When he opened them again, Gideon was standing much closer, and he seemed much larger, and the club seemed a little darker. "Thank you," he murmured.

A strong hand came around and cupped Jesse's ass, tugging him against Gideon's broader frame until their cocks rubbed against each other through their pants. Gideon licked a trail from Jesse's chin to his ear, stopping to whisper, "There is no safe word here, boy. For the next few hours, I'm going to fuck every hole you have, and then share you with whoever I see fit so that they can fuck you, too. I have every intention to feed from you at least once, and if it suits my mood, I'll allow anybody who asks to have a taste, too. You won't argue, you won't hesitate, and most of all, you won't stop until I tell you to. Do you understand?"

Jesse was perfectly fine with most of that speech. He wanted Gideon to fuck him, and he wanted Gideon to bite him, and he didn't want to argue, hesitate, or stop. But sharing? Actually letting other vampires touch him, and fuck him, and even feed off him? Jesse hadn't been prepared for that, and his brain seemed to short-circuit at the very idea. Gideon wouldn't let anybody hurt him, he firmly believed that, but how could he hang on to any sense of self, how could he continue working to fight and kill vampires, if he spent his spare time as some sort of vampire whore?

But it was Gideon's business—in every sense of the word. And if Gideon didn't see it as a problem, and if Gideon was going to protect him, and take him home, and if he was Gideon's, then he would push those thoughts out of his mind.

"Yes, I do," Jesse answered clearly.

Gideon nipped at his earlobe with blunt teeth, sending a fresh shiver straight to Jesse's cock. "That's my boy," he murmured. "Now let's go have fun."

Jess trailed after Gideon as he led them away from the bar and toward one of the few unoccupied couches. Gideon lounged against its plush cushions, dropping the leash for the first time since entering the club, and stretched his arms across the sofa's back.

"Strip," he ordered in no uncertain tone.

Jesse looked around. They were already attracting curious glances, and soon the vampires, like sharks, would be surrounding him, waiting for the first drop of blood. The image wouldn't leave him as he unbuttoned the shirt and pants. He kicked off his shoes and quickly removed the clothes, placing them all on the couch beside Gideon. The vamps didn't move in for an attack, but they were there, behind him. He felt them watching him, every instinct screaming at him to run. He focused on Gideon and quelled that fear.

Gideon ignored the growing number of onlookers. He slid his gaze to where his hard cock jutted out from his body, lingering there for long seconds while Jesse tried not to fidget. "Very nice," he murmured.

It took a moment for Jess to realize that it was the first time Gideon had seen him since he'd shaved. A pleased flush spread over his skin.

"Down." When Jess obeyed the command without pause, getting on his knees between Gideon's legs, a faint smile curved Gideon's mouth. "I have lube in my pocket. Get it, get your ass good and slick, and then take my cock out. I want you in my lap like a good boy."

Jesse thought of the instructions in list form, mentally sorting each one and then checking them off. He stuck his hand into Gideon's tight pocket and pulled out the small bottle of lube. He realized his fingers were shaking ever-so-slightly, and he wondered if Gideon noticed the quiver, and if so, what Gideon thought about it.

He covered two fingers with the lube, wishing Gideon had chosen to stretch his ass himself. It had only been a week since Gideon had buried his fingers inside him, but it seemed like much longer. Taking a deep breath, he reached behind him and eased both fingers into his tight hole. His body vibrated in time with the pulsing music, and he tried to pretend Gideon's fingers were thrusting in and out of him.

"That's enough," Gideon said.

Jesse pulled his hand away immediately and straightened. He unzipped Gideon's pants and pulled his cock free, the rest of the club fading to silence as soon as he touched Gideon's velvety skin. He licked his lips, but Gideon took him by the hips and spun him around, so he couldn't deny the leering yellow eyes, the sneering, fangy smiles. Averting his eyes, he gripped the base of Gideon's cock, holding it in position. Taking a very deep breath, he slowly lowered himself onto Gideon's shaft, his body burning with each exquisite centimeter, until Gideon was buried in his ass to his root.

Gideon's sigh was accompanied by his hands reaching around Jesse's chest, pressing flat as he pulled Jess back against his body. It changed the angle of his cock inside him, and an electric tingle went to his balls. But it was nothing compared to the wet suction of Gideon's mouth as he worked at the exposed skin above the collar. As Gideon made his way upward, it forced Jesse to lean his head back on the vampire's shoulder.

In spite of their audience, nothing had ever felt so good. Gideon's arms around him, Gideon's cock inside him, Gideon's mouth on him…what else could possibly compare?

"You feel so fucking great," Gideon murmured. "I've been waiting all week to get back inside you. I even had to stay away today to make sure I didn't crack and fuck you before our date."

Jesse nodded, unsure he'd be able to form actual words, even if he felt comfortable talking. But he had a flash, a sudden image, of Gideon fucking him whenever the mood struck him, of Gideon forcing him to his knees, under his desk, night or day, of Gideon tying him to the bed, or a chair, or chaining him to the ceiling again. Gideon thrust forward then, and the combined images and physical sensation might have been enough to make him come, if the cock ring wasn't preventing it. He whimpered, his hand snaking around Gideon's neck, desperate for something solid to hold.

A rich chuckle reverberated through Gideon's body, making Jesse's resonate in kind. "Patience," he said. "I'm going to fuck you properly soon enough. And you're going to need to be holding on with both hands when that happens." One of the hands splayed across Jesse's chest slid down, over his abdomen, along his cock, to the soft balls below. "This is going to be so much better than before. Do you know why?"

Jesse shook his head. He was already so high-strung that he didn't know how he was going to have patience or do this all night. "No."

"Because this is just you and me. No weird poison to make me do it. It's me taking you for my own because that's what I want. All of me." His touch was hypnotic, circling Jesse's balls, circling a flat nipple. Jesse's head was spinning. "Do you understand the difference now, Jess?"

"God, yes," he whispered, and all the emotions that always lurked well below the surface tried to break free, but he smashed them back until the impulse to share passed. "Yes, I understand."

His answer seemed to satisfy Gideon, and he sank farther back into him as Gideon resumed kissing his neck. It didn't matter any more that there were vampires watching his every move, and it didn't matter that Gideon seemed content to stay still, cock buried balls deep, only occasionally twitching as if to remind Jess that he was still there. When he took Jesse's chin and turned his head toward him, Jess accepted his kiss with every ounce of hunger and need he had for Gideon. He only hoped Gideon understood as well.

A rumbling voice cut through the spell.

"So who's the new toy, Gideon?"

Gideon licked Jesse's lips one last time before turning to look at the vampire who'd dared to speak up. He was big, bigger than Gideon, with a shaved head and sunken brown eyes. Dried blood clung to the corner of his mouth, and the bulge in his worn Levi's made Jesse's ass clench.

"Isn't he pretty?" Gideon replied. "I found him attached to my dick the other night. I decided I'd keep him around for awhile."

It was Gideon's casual response that really made him realize what was going on. He was just a toy to them. Nothing more. Far from frightening him, it made him feel free somehow.

The vampire licked his lips, his tongue pausing over the dried blood. "Pretty. What's better? His mouth or his ass?"

"Have you gone blind, Henry? You see this mouth, right?" Gideon ran his thumb over Jesse's lower lip before holding out his hand, palm up. "Come here. I'll feed you to him. He fucking loves that."

Jesse wasn't sure about that, but since nobody asked him his opinion, he simply watched Henry unzip his pants. His body was flooded with endorphins, and Jesse wasn't sure if it was fear or fresh arousal or if he'd ever be able to tell the difference between the two reactions again.

Henry's erection was...impressive. Impressive enough that Jesse was relieved Gideon wasn't going to let the vampire fuck him. He hoped. Gideon exhaled in his ear, his breath soft and oddly comforting, as he gripped Henry's cock.

Henry's knees were pressed to the edge of the couch as he leaned forward, following the pull of Gideon's hand. Jesse opened his mouth as it neared, but instead of slipping it inside, Gideon ran the dripping tip around his lips, smearing the pre-come until that was all he could smell or taste.

"Henry's got a nice cock, don't you think?" Gideon asked in his ear.

"Yes, he does," Jesse agreed obediently, but he wasn't lying. It was a nice cock, objectively speaking. How did Gideon know Henry by name? Had they fucked? Had they shared another...toy? He wanted to know, because the image the thought presented sent a current of electricity down his spine.

"I'd let him fuck you, but that would mean getting out of your ass and I'm not ready for that." A cool lick across his ear made Jess shiver. "Now open wide."

Jess did as instructed, and no sooner had his lips parted, Gideon was guiding the cock into his mouth, the velvety head sliding over his tongue. Gideon didn't let go until there was no more room for his hand on the thick shaft and then he just moved out of the way, easing back against the couch as Henry grasped either side of Jesse's head.

"Fuck his face," Gideon said. "And make sure you tell me if he uses his teeth. I've been looking for a good reason to discipline him all night."

Jesse didn't think he could avoid using his teeth. Henry's cock was too big, and Henry took Gideon's words to heart. There was no time to adjust, no time to linger over taste or texture, no time to become accustomed to the length and width. He was really nothing but a hole. He relaxed his jaw, relaxed his throat, tried to breathe through his nose, and clenched around Gideon's cock each time Henry drove into his mouth, his own cock aching in sympathy. His entire body throbbed in time to Henry's harsh rhythm.

"You like that, don't you, you little cockslut?" Henry's voice was as rough as his tempo, scraping over Jesse's bare skin. "That's right, take it, all the way...fuck, Gideon, you lucked out with this one. His mouth is fucking brilliant."

Though he no longer had Gideon against his back, Jess felt the unmistakable stroke of his hand along his spine. "Trust me," came the response. "I'm very well aware of how good he sucks cock."

Jesse didn't think Gideon could even compare what Henry was doing to him to what Jesse wanted to do for Gideon. He gripped Henry's thighs, digging his fingers into the denim covered muscle. Jesse didn't know how much time had passed, how many strokes Henry needed, how many thrusts and grunts. It seemed like an eternity and no time at all until the large vampire yanked his cock away from Jesse's mouth, only to coat his face with warm come.

Before he wiped it away, Gideon's arm was looped around his waist, yanking him back against his chest. When he grabbed Jesse's chin, Jess met Gideon's golden-eyed gaze for a split second before Gideon licked a wet trail along his cheek, catching some of the dripping fluid.

"Good boy," he heard Gideon murmur. Then their mouths were fused together, fangs slicing through the tender skin of his lower lip, as Gideon devoured him in a kiss.

The praise warmed him, and Gideon's mouth once again made the rest of the world disappear. Gideon sucked at his lips hungrily, pulling the blood from the small cut in thin threads. He was becoming accustomed to the taste of his own blood on Gideon's mouth.

When the kiss finally ended, Jesse gasped for breath, desperately taking in as much air as he could. Henry was still hovering above them, like he expected something more.

"You've had your turn," Gideon said, a note of irritation creeping into his voice. He waved a hand in dismissal. "Now get out of the way. You're holding up the line."

Though he scowled, Henry headed off, a skinny little guy already scrambling up to fill his place. Gideon repeated the process, taking the vampire's dick in hand and guiding it to Jesse's waiting mouth, over and over and over again. Every time, the new vampire would pull out at the last second, spraying Jesse's face and chest with come, and every time, Gideon ended it with a kiss, cleaning away some of the sticky fluid to share with Jess. The only variation lay in how long Gideon kissed him, each instance longer than the one before, until, after the sixth or seventh blow job—Jess had long ago given up counting—Gideon waved off the next recipient.

"Back off," he growled. His arm grew rigid where it was clamped around Jess' abdomen, holding him still. "You've all had your turn. It's mine now."

Jesse sucked his breath in sharply. Gideon's cock was still buried in his ass, which had long ago surpassed the realm of pleasure for something beyond torturous. He wanted Gideon to turn him over, pin him against the couch, and finally fuck him and—*ohpleasegod*—let him come. He couldn't say anything about it, of course, but maybe Gideon would read his mind and take some pity on him.

The vampires retreated, though they only moved far enough out of the way to give Gideon room to rise if he wanted. He relaxed his hold on Jesse's waist and said, "Stand up. I want you on your back when I split you open."

Jesse rose slowly, still feeling stretched, still feeling Gideon inside of him, even after they were completely separated. The crowd watched with hungry eyes and growls. Gideon gestured to the couch, and Jesse lay down eagerly. The room looked different from the new angle. Gideon looked different. Jesse bent one knee, and dropped his other foot to the floor, his legs splayed.

Shifting to kneel between Jesse's legs, Gideon took his cock in hand and stroked it, long, languorous pulls that matched the gleam in his eye. He tilted his head as his gaze swept down Jesse's body.

"You should see your ass right now, Jess," he said. "You're all open and red, and if I didn't want to fuck you so badly, I'd be down there right now with my tongue buried in your hole."

"I'd come the second you touched me with your tongue," Jesse said thickly.

Gideon grinned. "Now that sounds like a challenge. Maybe I should tighten that ring up a little."

"Please don't." Jesse almost gurgled the words. "Please."

The smile faded, to be replaced by something darker, a feral hunger that sank into Jesse's bones. "Oh, I do love it when you beg," Gideon murmured. He let go of his cock and fell forward, hovering over Jess eye-to-eye as he propped himself up on either side of Jesse's body. Angling his hips, he let the wet head drag along until it slipped below Jesse's sac, stopping at his waiting hole. "Think there's enough slick left for me to pound into you?"

"Yes, yes, please, please, yes," the words came in an unguarded rush. "Slick, stretched, ready for you. Please."

Slowly, Gideon pressed forward, sinking into Jesse's waiting flesh. A shudder rippled visibly through Gideon, but he didn't stop, didn't falter, continued to move at that excruciating pace until Jess thought Gideon was never going to finish, that he'd never feel the heavy brush of the vampire's balls against his skin. His hands itched to mold over Gideon's back, but he was still unsure of how much affection he could show for Gideon. Instead, he closed his eyes in an attempt to control himself and stifle the urge.

Gideon stopped. "Jess. Open your eyes."

Jesse opened his eyes immediately, his face twisting in a silent plea. He realized the heavy breathing in his ears wasn't his own. It was a collected, unneeded sigh from their audience. Jesse didn't care. He gripped the back of the couch with one hand, the other falling to his side. His body tried to force the issue, but instead of pushing his hips forward, he remained still and waited.

"Don't close them again," Gideon ordered. He reached beyond Jesse's peripheral vision, but when his hand returned to view, the leash was coiled around his fingers. His body tensed, and though Jesse prepared himself for the torturous re-entry, Gideon surprised him. With a vicious thrust, he slammed into Jesse's ass until his balls slapped against the flesh.

The angle brought Gideon's cock directly against his prostate. Jesse gritted his teeth, biting back a shout, the tendons in his neck and shoulders standing out. If the cock ring wasn't there, he would have exploded at that moment. As it was, he wondered if his body, if his skin would actually split from the growing pressure. He thought he might be saying something, something about needing more, but he wasn't sure if he was actually forming the words, or just thinking them.

Gideon was moving, pistoning in and out his ass, lowering himself until they touched, chest to chest. Fangs skimmed over his skin, and the distinct sting meant that Gideon had drawn blood. But Jess was too aware of that dangerous mouth at his ear, and shivered as the words were sent in cascading whispers through his veins.

"The others can talk all they want, but at the end of the day, you're *my* cockslut, Jess. Mine. Mine to do with as I please, to fuck as I want, to eat as I want. Because I think you want it even more than I do. You *want* to be on your knees. You *want* me to mark you, to stretch your ass out so that it's the perfect shape for my cock. But you wanna know what I want right now? I want to hear you admit it. Tell me you're a slut for me and me alone. Do that, and I'll let you come."

Jesse was in a smoky, red haze. He'd say or agree to anything at that point, and all Gideon wanted from him was the truth. "Yours. Your slut...your anything, anything you want. Only you, Gideon." *Always.*

Gideon's thrusts grew ragged and uneven, and though Jesse knew there was an entire crowd watching every inch of their bodies, all he was aware of was the weight of Gideon pushing him into the couch, and the slide of his cashmere shirt over his chest, and the sparks that coursed through him every time Gideon slammed into his prostate. But when he thought he'd have to resort to begging again, Gideon's hand moved, somehow slipping between their bodies to find the leather holding him back. With one deft move, he unsnapped the cock ring.

Jesse grabbed Gideon's shoulders, giving in to the urge to touch him. He teetered on the fine edge for one more stroke, but as soon as Gideon was deep inside him again, he became unhinged. He wrapped his arms around Gideon, their bodies pressed together, Jesse's cock jerking, covering his stomach and Gideon with come. He somehow remembered not to close his eyes, but he shouted until his sore throat was on fire, and the leather collar around his neck felt tight and restricting around his sweaty throat.

Gideon's lips curled into a hungry snarl, and without breaking his rhythm into Jess, he let go of the leash and pushed up the collar, scraping it across slick skin until the puncture marks from his first bite were exposed. He struck, unerringly and sure, fangs sinking through fragile skin to leave Jess trembling and scorched. His hips jerked only one more time before Jess felt the flood of come coating his ass, blast after blast as Gideon drank as he had promised Jess he would do.

It didn't last nearly as long as it had the first time, though it still felt like the room was spinning when Gideon retracted his fangs. Jess was saved from having to be coherent by the coppery press of Gideon's mouth to his, and he clung to him, momentarily sated and content, as he returned the kiss.

"Thank you," Jesse breathed, his lips moving against Gideon's. "Thank you. That was...really...wonderful."

"Just wait. The night's not over yet."

He felt bereft when Gideon pulled away, ready to yank him back and continue the kisses that made the world vanish. But Gideon surprised him by staying pressed to his body, choosing instead only to slide down Jesse's length. He stopped at his stomach, and Jess gasped at the first touch of Gideon's tongue. Lifting his head, he watched Gideon eat away every trace of his come. At some point between his lips and his abdomen, Gideon had shifted back to his human visage, and now he nipped at Jesse's skin with blunt teeth, not stopping even after it was clear. He simply moved lower, pushing Jesse's knees up to lift his open ass off the couch.

"Think you can hold back from coming the second I touch you now?" Gideon taunted.

Jess caught his breath as Gideon's dark head lowered. The first touch was a gentle swipe around the ring of muscle, soothing some of the burn of being stretched for so long. The second was a long lick up and down the crack, ending with Gideon sucking Jesse's balls into his mouth. But the third touch was back at his ass, and this time, Gideon clamped his mouth around the hole and sank his tongue inside.

The ceiling spun around above him, and he gripped the cushion to keep from flying off the couch. If they had been in the privacy of Gideon's apartment, he would have buried his hand in Gideon's hair, but as the circle of vampires closed in around them, he decided to keep his hands to himself. Slowly, his blurred vision filled with fangs, flashing yellow eyes, and then cocks. Jesse saw them, but they were inconsequential. Gideon's fingers were bruising on his thighs, and he thrust his tongue furiously, stoking the fire through his veins until his cock was hard again.

When Gideon lifted his head, it was both agony and a relief. His ass clenched convulsively as he spied the slight bob of Gideon's thick cock, but Gideon chose instead to sit back and tuck himself into his leather pants.

"I'm going to leave the ring off," he said. His mouth was shiny from the come he'd just licked from Jesse's ass. Jess couldn't stop staring at it, wondering if he dared to kiss Gideon and get a taste. "But if you come before I tell you to, you'll wear it for a week."

Jesse nodded. "I understand," he rasped. It occurred to him that if he could talk the next day, it'd be a bloody miracle. "Gideon...I need...can I use the restroom?"

Snorts of amusement and a muffled *fucking humans* drifted to his ears. Gideon ignored all of them and nodded, standing up and holding his hand out expectantly. It took Jess a moment to understand what he wanted, but when he saw the leather leash trailing over the side of the couch, it came together. Silently, he picked it up and held it out.

"Leave your clothes here," Gideon instructed, coiling the leash around his hand. "I want everyone to see how well fucked you are while I'm walking you to the bathroom."

Jesse shuffled behind Gideon as he slowly guided him through the club. He realized Gideon really was showing off, and they were definitely attracting more attention. Jess didn't assume they were staring at him, necessarily, not when they could be staring at Gideon. He was shocked by his own lack of shame. He didn't feel the least bit self-conscious, even when Gideon yanked sharply on the leash and tugged him down a narrow corridor.

They passed a scrawny girl smoking in the hall, and Gideon jerked his head back toward the main room. She went scurrying off, and they continued forward, stopping when they reached a door near its end.

"It's a private bathroom," Gideon said. "Which means I don't have to go in with you. But I'm going to wait right outside for you to come out again." He pushed Jess almost gently into the wall, his fingers gliding along Jesse's arms. "It's not safe for me to leave you unprotected."

No, it wouldn't be. Jesse knew full well they'd descend on him like bull sharks on a whale carcass if Gideon left him for a second. As soon as Gideon pulled the door shut, Jesse perched on the edge of the toilet, his hands shaking violently.

"Oh...shit. Shit, shit, shit." Jesse murmured. How many times had he nearly blurted that he loved Gideon? How many times? He knew he couldn't say it, especially not then, and probably not ever. So why did it keep almost happening? And what was wrong with him, that being treated that way, in front of a bunch of blood-thirsty, scary vampires, brought those feelings closer to the surface than any other time?

Jesse stood up and walked over to the sink. He knew if he wasted too much time, Gideon would come in and drag him out. Hoping Gideon wouldn't mind, he ran the hot water and washed his hands, arms, and mouth. Not his entire face—no sense in treading too far over the line—but all the dried come and blood around his swollen lips was scrubbed away.

He looked up and caught sight of his own reflection. He didn't look like himself. Jesse had never seen that stranger. Maybe it was the stranger who wanted to shout his love for Gideon at the top of his lungs.

"Say it once, and get it out of your system," Jesse instructed his reflection. The stranger's head nodded and whispered, "I love you, Gideon."

After splashing his face one more time, he emerged from the small room.

Gideon seemed to unfold from the darkness, his eyes black pools in his pale face, and stalked toward him to catch the leash that dangled down his chest. Before Jess made a sound, Gideon pushed him against the wall, pinning him with first his hips, then his shoulders, and finally his mouth. It was the kiss Jess had wanted on the couch, the taste of come still strong on Gideon's tongue, but it was different than the others, purposeful and possessive and leaving Jess shaking long before he pulled away.

"Do you know how hot it is seeing everybody in here want a piece of you?" Gideon murmured. "I *had* to fuck you. I thought my dick was going to explode watching you suck everybody else's."

"I imagined they were all you," Jesse admitted. "I'll do whatever you want but..." His hand rested on the bulge in Gideon's pants. "This is...you are all I want."

Gideon pushed against his hand, encouraging Jesse to mold his fingers over his cock and palm its length through the leather. "And what if I want to watch you get fucked? What if I want to see you drowning in come, with all these pretty colors on your skin?"

Jesse rotated his wrist, massaging his firm erection and wishing the damned pants weren't in the way. "Then I want that, too."

He caught the smug smile as Gideon stepped back and broke the contact. "A natural born slut," Gideon commented. "Those all-night research parties you keep trying to get me to attend just got a whole lot more promising."

"For you and me both," Jesse murmured, as Gideon took the leash again.

The hall was dark and comparatively quiet, and his senses weren't prepared for the renewed onslaught of light and music. Gideon gave a sharp tug, nearly pulling him off his feet, but he caught himself and straightened. He expected Gideon to lead him back to the couch, but he turned, walking the opposite direction.

They only went a few feet before Gideon came to an abrupt halt. The face he turned back to Jess was unyielding again, not the one he was coming to know when it was just the two of them, but the one presented to the other vampires in the club.

"On your hands and knees, boy," he ordered. "Nobody can see how good and stretched your ass is if you walk."

Forcing himself not to think about what he might stick his hands in as he crawled around on the floor, he dropped to his knees. The leash was long enough to accommodate Jesse's position, and he felt more than a little overwhelmed by his new view of the world. Gideon began to walk again, not even sparing him a second glance, and Jesse had no choice but to follow, his eyes focused on Gideon's shoes.

Cool, pale hands reached out to graze along Jesse's sides as they wove around the couches. They scratched across skin, petted his flank, pinched when he got too close, but Gideon didn't slow or pause to allow any of them a chance to linger. Just as he'd done when they'd gone to the bathroom, Gideon was parading Jesse around, and a swell of pride rose inside him at the thought that the man he loved wanted to brag about having Jess at his cock and call. It made crawling easier. It made everything easier.

His knees were starting to hurt when Gideon finally stopped, and Jesse lifted his head to see what had prompted him to do so. In front of them, a vampire couple was sharing a girl who looked barely out of her teens, their fangs buried in either side of her neck as they fondled her breasts and pussy. They looked up at Gideon's approach, and the woman smiled, her mouth stained in scarlet.

"Gideon! Where have you been? We haven't seen you in ages. Everybody's been wondering about you."

Gideon shrugged. Even the slight gesture tugged at the collar around Jesse's throat. "Been busy." He nodded toward the girl who lolled semi-conscious in their arms. "Looks like you could use some fresh blood."

Two sets of golden eyes turned to Jess at the same time. Hunger lurked in both of them, but it was the woman who turned a pout back to Gideon.

"You should've brought him by before we ate," she said. "He looks yummy."

"Oh, Jess is good for more than feeding." He jerked on the leash, forcing Jesse to crawl forward to his side. "Show Monique and Eric what you can do, boy."

Jesse looked up with confusion, but Gideon apparently didn't plan to give him further instruction. As he crawled over to the couch, they dumped the girl to the ground without a second thought, and he hesitated. Would she be okay? Was she there for the same reason he was, or had she been lured into this place and attacked? He reached out to touch her pulse briefly, satisfied with the strength of it against her thin skin. If Gideon noticed, he didn't say anything.

"Come here, pretty boy," Monique cooed, spreading her legs. Blood had dripped down her chest, and there were fresh bite marks on her thighs. It was clear what she wanted from him. "That's it. I want to feel your hot little mouth. Why should the guys have all the fun?"

As she spoke, she gripped the back of his head and guided his mouth to her pussy.

The smell of blood was stronger between her legs, but Jess ignored it to focus on her swollen lips. With the tip of his tongue, he licked a path around the soft flesh, not daring to go near her clit or opening until the hand on his head grew firmer. Then he circled the sensitive flesh, only catching it between his teeth when she ground her pussy against his mouth.

A hand too large to be Gideon's smoothed down Jesse's spine. "He's already been fucked," Eric complained.

"Only by me," Gideon said. "He's still good and tight."

"Fuck him, Eric," Monique said. She scissored her legs around Jesse's shoulders, pinning him in place. "I'll hold him steady for you."

61

Jesse braced himself without diverting his attention from Monique. He knew it wouldn't be too bad, since he was still slick from Gideon's come and tongue, but he didn't know if he was prepared for a stranger to go that far. Until he remembered the tone of Gideon's voice when he said he wanted to see somebody else fuck him. Though he couldn't see Gideon, he imagined him watching them with half-closed eyes, his cock straining against his pants.

Strong hands pulled at his cheeks, spreading him open. "God, I love fucking humans," Eric murmured, before driving the length of his cock in Jess' ass. He grunted, Monique's legs the only thing keeping him from falling forward. "They're so fucking hot."

A shadow blocked some of the flashing strobe above, and Jesse saw Gideon sit down on the couch next to Monique. Casually, he threw an arm over her shoulders, but his dark eyes locked on Jesse's.

"Bruise him," he ordered. "Everybody's being too fucking easy on him tonight."

Eric laughed, a mean sound, and his hands went to Jesse's hips. "Gladly."

Jesse whimpered in the back of his throat as pain flowered through his body. He knew he'd have ten finger-shaped marks on his hips for a long time, and Eric used enough force to make his teeth rattle. But looking at Gideon focused Jess, and soon pleasure began to overtake the pain, moving with it side by side.

Monique moaned, her strong thighs surprisingly hot around his face. It was difficult to concentrate on his task while it felt like he was being split in two, but he pulled her clit between his teeth, alternately biting and sucking. Supporting himself on only one hand, he sought out her opening with his other and thrust his fingers into her wet channel.

"Oh, fuck," Monique said. Fingers laced through his hair, but they were too broad to be hers, and Eric's still gripped his hips as he pounded into Jesse's ass. Jess looked up through his lashes to see Gideon leaning forward, and the lust burning in his face was enough to spur him to drive his fingers into Monique's pussy harder, to squeeze around the cock in his ass a little tighter. Eric shouted before pulling out, and splash after splash of warm come landed on Jesse's back.

"You're so fucking gorgeous," Gideon murmured.

Gideon's words stunned Jess, but the tightening of Monique's legs around his neck warned him not to stop. How could one simple sentence fill him with such a sense of elation? The words echoed in his head as he moaned and hummed against Monique's clit, vibrating the swollen flesh with his lips. He curled his fingers, scraping against her G-spot, and sunk one of his incisors into her clit. Monique screamed, thrashing around him with surprising force, and then her legs fell away.

By the time Jesse looked up again, Gideon was no longer on the couch. He had only started to turn his head to look for him when a tug on the leash pulled him upright, and he stood there, Eric's come dripping over his buttocks as Gideon pressed behind him.

"I told you my boy was good," he said. "He tastes even better."

His hand snaked around Jesse's hip, grasping him at the base of his cock. The squeeze was painful, blocking out the immediate urge to come, but that was eclipsed by the rake of fangs along his shoulder. Jess barely had time to take a deep breath before Gideon sank his teeth into the tight sinew at his nape.

Monique and Eric both looked at him with greedy, gluttonous eyes, but Jesse didn't even wince. He had no doubt that if either tried to touch him at that moment, Gideon would make them sorry.

"I'm still getting my taste," Monique murmured, sliding off the couch to kneel in front of him.

Jesse watched her warily, but she didn't touch him. Gideon took a long, slow swallow, making his head spin, and began stroking his length. His ass throbbed, his balls throbbed, his body throbbed, and Gideon felt solid behind him. Another long drag, and another, and another. The world began to blur. Jesse's eyes went to the nearly unconscious girl, and he hoped in a distant way that he wasn't going to pass out, too, but even if he could tell Gideon to stop, it was too much, he wouldn't have said a word.

On the fourth swallow, as the blurred edges turned dark, Jesse erupted, shouting Gideon's name. Monique opened her mouth, catching the arcs of come with a greedy tongue.

The fangs disappeared, and Gideon's mouth slid to Jesse's jaw, his strong arms holding him firmly upright. "They're going to talk about you here for weeks," he murmured. "And they're all going to say what I already know. That you're absolutely amazing, Jess."

Oh, Jesus, God, I love you. He closed his eyes, knowing that nobody was paying any attention to his face, but not wanting anybody to see the unhinged emotions in his eyes. He sagged against Gideon, wishing he would take them home. Tilting his head back, he looked up, hoping Gideon would made the decision without prompting from him.

"Ooo, bring him here for me to clean up," Monique cooed.

"I know you," came Gideon's annoyed response. "You'll bite him as soon as he's close enough."

"So?" Her laugh was clear and chilling. "Lighten up, Gideon. Go see Henry. He'll fix you so you won't even care."

Gideon stiffened behind him. "What do you mean, he'll fix me? What's Henry into now?"

Eric flopped down on the couch next to Monique. "The best shit, I'm telling you. This stuff is so good, all you have to do is *touch* it and you're flying."

Jesse stumbled as Gideon let him go, swaying dizzily as he struggled not to topple over. Gideon didn't seem to notice, too absorbed in searching the club—for Henry, Jess assumed. Everything about him had gone steely, and the hands that had been stroking Jesse were now balled into fists.

"Let me guess," Gideon said. "He's dealing out of a warehouse on Palm."

"How'd you know that?"

"Don't ask," Gideon muttered. He grabbed Jesse's leash, yanking it a little too hard. "Come on. We're getting out of here."

CHAPTER 7

Though he led Jesse back to the couch to get his clothes, Gideon's mind was elsewhere, locked in the maelstrom both of what he'd learned and what he'd brought Jess into. He knew Henry was bad news, trafficking in everything from sex peddling to drugs alongside the humans he co-existed with, but he had never suspected that he'd branch out into substances aimed at the demon world. The drug Monique and Eric described sounded exactly like what Gideon had encountered, and the fact that Henry was working out of the same warehouse where he'd touched it only confirmed that fact.

He hadn't seen Henry when he'd scanned the club, though. And the last thing Gideon wanted was to leave Jess alone while he searched for him.

God. Jess. He'd *brought* him here. Yes, he knew exactly what he'd been doing, but for all its appearances, Sangre was a safe environment. As long as a human had a clear master, and as long as that master wasn't fucking stupid and left him vulnerable, all that happened within Sangre's walls was pleasure. Sex, and bloodplay, and more sex, and the occasional blackout when someone got a little too greedy in feeding. All Gideon had wanted was to expose Jess to the darker alleys of his life, to see if he would turn tail and run or embrace the pleasure to be had in giving himself over. Toss in the opportunity to try and spot Toby Richards' vampire girlfriend, and it had seemed like a no-brainer as a date option.

Henry's dealings changed everything, though. If vampires here were using whatever it was that erased all of Gideon's inhibitions, Sangre was no longer the safe haven he thought it was. Gideon could protect Jess, but not against a mob determined for more. And if Jesse's safety wasn't guaranteed, he wouldn't take the risk.

He finally looked at Jess when they reached the couch. His lean body was streaked with blood transferred from Monique, Eric's fresh come on his back, and the drying come he'd missed cleaning away in the bathroom. His hair was a riot of dark waves, and his mouth was red and swollen. He looked absolutely nothing like the perfectly groomed man who showed up for work every day, always five minutes early.

Gideon thought he had never been so entranced by a person's duality as he was with Jesse's. He couldn't let him get hurt, not now, not ever.

When Jess began to get dressed, Gideon shook his head. "Over here," he said, nodding toward the bar.

Jess frowned, but didn't argue, following Gideon's lead as they navigated through the throng to the less-crowded bar area. Gideon motioned for him to step off to the side, releasing the leash, and watched him out of the corner of his eye as he called over the bartender.

"I was wondering," he said. "Have you seen Tricia around tonight?"

The bartender's brows drew together into a thick line as he considered the question. "You mean Henry's Tricia?"

Gideon's stomach sank. "Yeah. Henry's Tricia."

The bartender shook his head. "She hasn't been in for awhile. A couple weeks maybe."

Since Toby's death. Gideon wasn't sure if that was a good thing or a really, really bad thing.

"Did Henry take off already?"

"Who knows? Ever since he started bringing in that obsidian shit, he's never in one place for any amount of time. If you don't see him out on the floor, he could be out back, or upstairs in his office, or gone. That's Henry."

"Yeah." Gideon looked back over the crowd. "That's Henry."

Jess was done getting dressed, waiting expectantly a few feet away. When Gideon turned to him, he held out the leash for Gideon to take, his blue eyes burning.

Gideon's smile was soft as he took it. "Let's get you home."

The air was actually hotter outside the club, the sultry night clinging to Gideon's skin when they stepped outside the door. Behind him, Jesse took a deep breath, and out of the corner of his eye, he saw Jesse's grimace of pain. It could have been the result of any number of things, but before Gideon asked, the valet was pressing his keys into his palm.

"Thank you, sir, have a good evening."

Gideon nodded and led Jesse to the car. As soon as Jess slid into the passenger seat, with another grimace, Gideon unsnapped the leash from his collar and tossed it in the backseat. Jesse lifted the corner of his mouth in a half-smile, but he didn't speak until Gideon was in the car and pulling away from the club.

"I may not have my full faculties, but what's going on, Gideon?" His words were hoarse and low. "Who's Tricia?"

Gideon's hands were tight on the steering wheel. "Toby Richards' girlfriend. I was hoping she'd be here tonight." They pulled to a stop at a red light, and Gideon twisted to grab a backpack tucked behind the passenger seat. He handed it over to Jess. "There's bottles of water in there. It'll help your throat until we get home and I can make you some hot tea."

"Thanks." He opened one and downed the entire thing in several long, greedy gulps. "So, Henry, who I'm assuming is the owner of the club, is dealing something, probably the substance we're looking for, out of the warehouse where we found the knob, and that's linked to a girl, probably a vampire, named Tricia, who was dating Toby, and also is clearly connected to this Henry fellow?"

"Part owner," Gideon corrected. "That's why he was first in line to get at you. He considers Sangre his turf, even if he's only one of three investors. But yeah, you're right about the rest of it. I thought if I found Monique, I could hit her up to point Tricia out to me, so we could ask the girl questions about Toby." The light turned green, and Gideon eased the car through the intersection. "Monique's pretty much the Hedda Hopper of the demon set here in town."

"Gideon, you didn't know about his connection to the warehouse until tonight, did you?"

"No. Henry's a rough character, but he's never dealt in demon drugs before. This is new territory. And all I thought I'd get out of tonight was a chance to interrogate Tricia and find out what really happened to Toby." Unbidden, his mouth curved into a smile. "And watch you get thoroughly fucked, of course."

"Why didn't you tell me any of this?"

"Because I didn't want you involved. Just like I didn't like you going to the warehouse." Out of the corner of his eye, he caught Jess still regarding him with that annoyed frown that invariably preceded an argument of some sort, and Gideon sighed in frustration. "Obsidian makes vampires unpredictable," he said. "I almost killed you when I was on it. I am not going to see you get hurt by getting stuck in the middle of this case."

"So, you're telling me I'm not allowed to do my actual job, but taking me to a club full of vampires that could have just as easily had access to the stuff is acceptable?"

"I told you. I didn't *know* about Henry's involvement. I didn't even know there was more of this shit floating around. I thought if I could get the answers Richards wanted about Toby on my own, I could contain this and keep you out of harm's way."

"But you thought Tricia would be there," Jess argued. "And you knew, or at least strongly suspected, that Tricia had something to do with the drugs. What if she had been there and she was carrying the drugs? I wouldn't have even had a warning." His hands curled into fists on his lap, and every tense line of his body betrayed his anger. "Are there any other cases I'm forbidden from working on? Should I just not draw a paycheck for this month since, apparently, I have nothing to contribute to this very serious, very dangerous situation that could directly lead to more deaths?"

"Damn it, Jess, stop making this a bigger deal than it is!"

Gideon saw their turn a fraction of a second too late, and the tires squealed as he jerked the wheel in order to make it. Jesse's body slammed into the car door, his wince of pain audible, and a flash of guilt eased Gideon's stranglehold on the steering wheel.

"I got you out of there as soon as I realized there was a definite threat," he said, his voice more calm. "And, yes, I'm beginning to realize that taking you to Sangre at all was a huge mistake."

"It is a big deal," Jesse said softly. "I thought we had a partnership. That means we share information and we trust each other. If I've been wrong all this time, then you need to tell me, so I know what to expect. And what do you mean taking me to Sangre at all was a big mistake?"

Gideon's jaw locked shut. Jesse's description of their relationship fit everything Gideon had believed, prior to that first night he'd fucked his best friend in an alley. Seen through more rational eyes, he understood how his actions since then might be construed differently. Was his desire for a new kind of relationship with Jess ruining the foundation they'd already had? Gideon knew he was possessive, he knew he was protective. He'd always been that way, because when you were stronger and outlived your friends and loved ones, that's what you did to keep them around as long as possible.

Before all this, he would've shared the information he had with Jess, without pause or second thought. Was Gideon treating Jess differently because of his own fear of losing him somehow? He suspected the answer was a resounding yes.

"Maybe this thing between you and me isn't such a good idea," he said. "Maybe we should just chalk tonight up as a big mistake, and go back to the way things were. Clearly, trying to change things is fucking with our professional relationship."

"No, sorry, you don't get to make that decision. You don't get to put me to the test that way, and ask me to do things that I have never done before, or would ever do for anybody else, only to decide it was a mistake. We can't go back to the way things were now." Jesse sighed. "Gideon, do you trust me?"

"Of course, I do. But, Jess…please don't think you failed any kind of test tonight. You were spectacular back there." He desperately wanted to reach out and touch Jess, but after everything, he didn't believe he had the right. "*I* was the one who failed."

"I know you think you were protecting me," Jesse said, his earlier anger replaced by the sort of long-suffering patience that Gideon had become accustomed to. "But I don't need you to do that. I didn't need you to do it before, and I don't need it now. We work so well together because you don't have to shield me from the world…" He touched his arm, "And I don't need you to shield me from who you are, either."

When Gideon didn't immediately respond, Jess sighed and settled back in his seat. They continued on in silence for several blocks, candied neon flickering faintly through the blacked windows. Gideon knew Jess was waiting for him to say something, but frankly, he wasn't sure what he *could* say. Jess always found fresh ways of surprising him. He wasn't sure he deserved that.

They were only a few blocks from his apartment when it grew too oppressive for Gideon. "So what was it you'd never done before?" he asked, hoping like hell Jess would follow his lead and drop the entire matter.

"I'm not going to answer that question until you tell me what you want from me. And then I'll tell you anything you want, in great detail if you'd like."

Gideon snorted. "You never ask the easy questions, do you?"

"No, I don't. My teachers used to hate me."

"Obviously not the ones you got on your knees for. Who could hate somebody with as talented a mouth as yours?"

"Stop trying to get away from the subject, Gideon. I'll tell you about which teachers...liked...me more than others, *after* you answer me."

Sighing, Gideon pulled the car into the parking structure, rolling gently down the slope to the lower levels. "I want my best friend," he said quietly. "I want the guy who waits up until I drag in at dawn with my back in ribbons from being thrown through a windshield, and then stays up another two hours to help bandage me up. I want the guy who's always there when I need him, who always has the answer I didn't realize I was looking for." He pulled into his parking space, killing the engine before shifting to meet Jesse's steady gaze. "And, yeah, I want the guy who'll beg me to fuck him until he can't sit down and then gets on his knees to worship my cock until his ass is ready for me again. And I want to make sure that none of those guys ever, *ever* gets hurt."

"In order for me to be any of those guys, or all of those guys, you need to *trust* me, and be honest with me, or it won't work. If you can do that, I'll go inside with you now. If not, then you should take me back to my own place."

The words made him choke. "If I take you home, you're going to end up quitting, aren't you? That's what you said before."

"What's it going to be, Gideon?"

Jess wasn't denying what Gideon feared. That left only one answer.

"Then I trust you," he said. "Because losing you is not an option."

Jesse chuckled. "I would have preferred to hear you trust me because I'm brilliant and capable, but I suppose that'll do, too."

There was more Gideon wanted to say, like how brilliant and capable he thought Jesse was, or it wasn't so much a matter of trusting Jess as it was not trusting others, but Gideon held his tongue. He leaned across the space separating them, cupped his hand behind Jesse's neck, and pulled him close in order for their lips to meet in a brief, hard kiss.

"Let's go upstairs," he said. "I have a sponge and a shower that's got your name all over it."

Jesse smiled. "That's the best thing I've heard all night."

Jesse followed him out of the garage like he was still being led by the leash, but it didn't take long for Gideon to realize that Jesse wasn't still performing his role. His high from the sex had obviously faded, leaving nothing but actual bruises and sore muscles, but Jesse didn't say a word about it.

As soon as they reached the apartment, Jesse started stripping, leaving a trail of clothes from the front door to the bathroom.

CHAPTER 8

From the kitchen, Gideon listened to the distant sound of the shower, its rhythmic hum soothing even though he wasn't the one under the spray. There had been a moment when Jess had reached the doorway, when he had glanced back to meet Gideon's eyes, that he'd been tempted to ignore his earlier offer of hot tea for Jesse's throat and shove him to the wall to fuck him then and there. But Gideon had turned away, heading to the kitchen without a word. Jess didn't want to be treated any differently, so that's what he was going to do. He gave Jess privacy when he needed it. Tonight would be no different.

He poured the boiling water from the kettle into the teapot, stirring absently as he mulled over the night's events. He had no fucking clue what to do next. Lucas Richards wanted answers about Toby's death, but everything led back to Henry, who was the last person Gideon wanted to tangle with. And then there was this thing with Jess—this glorious, terrifying thing that had him zigging when he should be zagging. He'd almost lost Jess tonight. All because he tried to protect him. And while he'd meant it when he said he'd try and trust Jess, Gideon knew it was much easier said than done. Every instinct he had said to keep Jess away from danger. Gideon had no clue how he was going to ignore them.

The shower was still going after he'd poured out the tea, and Gideon walked over to the closed door, picking up Jesse's discarded clothes on the way. "Jess?" he called out. "You all right in there?"

There was no answer. Perhaps Jess hadn't heard him.

Gideon pushed the door open and was immediately wrapped in waves of steam. He blinked against the fog as he entered, hesitating when his gaze settled on the shower. Through the translucent glass, he saw Jess standing motionless beneath the spray. His dark head was bowed as he braced himself against the wall, and the scalding water pounded against his shoulders to cascade down his back. He didn't even look up when Gideon entered.

"Jess?" he tried again.

Jesse turned his head slightly, his eyes unbelievably dark against the pallor of his skin. "I can't reach the middle of my back."

Gideon tried not to wince at what that implied. "Do you want some help?"

"I'd appreciate it. A second pair of eyes and hands can't hurt. I keep finding unexpected stains in the most interesting places."

Quickly, Gideon shed his clothes and pulled aside the glass door to climb inside. He'd planned to have a shower after Jess was asleep, but now was as good a time as any, he supposed. When he saw the purple bruises already rising to the surface of Jesse's skin, he hesitated for a fraction of a moment, torn between arousal at how prettily they peppered Jess' pale flesh and guilt that he hadn't thought to take better care of him sooner.

"Anyplace I should be careful with because it hurts too much?" he asked as he positioned himself behind Jesse.

"Don't stick anything in my ass and we should probably be okay," Jesse said dryly.

Well, he couldn't be any blunter than that, Gideon thought. Picking up the sponge Jess had discarded, he poured on a fresh dollop of shower gel, rubbing it in to work up a lather. Gently, he began washing Jesse's back, starting at his knotted shoulders and sweeping down the length in long, steady strokes.

"You never told me what was new to you tonight," Gideon said. "I mean, other than going to a vampire club. That, you already said."

"Well, I shattered my previous record for number of blow jobs given in one night," Jesse said. "Come to think of it, I shattered all my records. And I've never been involved in a threesome."

"Huh. That wasn't what I expected you to say."

Jesse's body shook in a silent chuckle. "What did you expect? I've also never been led around by a leash, and all my previous partners were the jealous sort, so there was never any sharing like that. Well, never any sharing that I told them about."

Gideon's brows shot up. "Sneaking around behind lovers' backs? Now I *definitely* didn't expect that." Unable to resist, he pressed closer, snaking a loose arm around Jesse's waist as he murmured in his ear. "Just don't do it with me, because I'll know. And if you think they were jealous…"

Jesse shivered. "It's not even a possibility. Ever. But, out of curiosity, what would you do?"

"Kill them," Gideon said without pause. He ran the sponge in lazy circles over Jesse's abdomen, feeling it twitch beneath the contact. "Then I'd chain you up and find new and delightful ways to make you hurt and beg for me, until you realize that you're mine and only mine."

"Oh. Well, that's good to know . But, I promise, Gideon, it's never going to happen."

The sponge got caught on a patch of dried come low on Jesse's hip, and Gideon pulled back in order to turn Jess around to face him. He knelt to his knees to begin washing the lower half of Jesse's body, and though it brought him eye level with Jesse's cock, he studiously ignored it. For now.

"Is this a first for you?" he asked. If they were going to continue, Gideon realized he needed to know how much Jesse had done before. "Being…punished, I mean."

"I experimented with light bondage and S&M before. I've always been…attracted to the idea of it, but it's not easy to find the right partner." Jess ran his fingers through Gideon's hair. "I tried a few clubs before when I was younger, but that didn't work out for me. So this is, by and large, entirely unexplored territory for me."

Pausing in his attentions, Gideon glanced up at Jess. "Then how do you know this is what you want?"

"It feels right. Every time you touch me, everything you do, it just feels right."

Gideon averted his eyes and returned to washing before his thoughts betrayed him. "I think we're very compatible," he said, instead of the far more fervent vows going through his head. "It helps that we know each other so well."

"We are," Jesse agreed, "and it does help." There was a long pause before he asked, "What was it like for you tonight? What does it do for you to see me…like that?"

The truth was a double-edged sword. Gideon was glad he was working on Jesse's calves and feet when it was asked. It meant it was all right not to meet his eyes when he replied.

"It excites me," he said. "Part of it is seeing you taking and giving so much pleasure. That's arousing, in and of itself. I've always thought you were gorgeous, Jess, and getting to see all of you..." He swallowed, trying to will down his growing erection. He'd promised Jess he wasn't going anywhere near his ass tonight, and after everything, he wasn't in the mood for jerking off. "The other part...I guess it's pride. Of ownership, if that makes sense. I mean, we're partners, I know that, I know I don't *own* you. But, while we're someplace like Sangre, for a few hours, I can pretend I do. I like knowing people are looking at you and hating me for being the one to take you home at the end of the night. That you respond like you do because of me." He shrugged. "I know it probably doesn't make much sense."

"It makes sense to me," Jesse said, his words almost lost under the roar of the shower. He pointed to the bruises on his upper-thighs. "Do you like to see me marked like this?"

Lifting his gaze meant seeing Jesse's thickening cock as well as the flowering colors adorning his skin. "Yes," Gideon admitted. "I'm still a vampire, you know. The only thing that would make it better is knowing that they were mine."

"Some of them might be." Jesse's fingers brushed over Gideon's head, face, and shoulders, like he couldn't stop himself from touching him. "I know that you do like them, and I know why. It's just...I'm curious about what makes you tick."

He shot Jess a crooked smile. "That's because you're a brainiac and can't stop with the quest for knowledge."

"And because it turns me on. Though that might have something to do with my brainiac status as well."

On impulse, Gideon leaned forward and brushed his mouth across the nearest bruise. He caught a rivulet of water with his tongue, and the slight contact brought goosebumps to the surface of Jesse's hip.

"Did you enjoy tonight?" he asked. "I know you're hurt, and I know we had that stupid fight in the car, but the rest of it. What did you think?"

"Yes, I did enjoy the rest of it. Quite a bit. I don't mind getting hurt. It'll heal, and modern pharmaceuticals are a wonderful thing—and it's worth it. When you fuck me too hard, or when Eric fucked me tonight, it should hurt enough to make me beg for you to stop. But it doesn't really hurt. It's...it's all just...sensation. And I guess it's my turn not to make sense."

But he was. And the more he said, the more Gideon wanted to take him in his arms and never let him go.

He chose instead to resume mouthing the bruises on his hips, sucking just enough at each one to make Jess feel it before moving on to the rest. Jesse's hand rested on the top of his head, not guiding Gideon but merely following his path. When Gideon felt his cock brush against his cheek, he noticed that Jess had grown completely hard again, his balls hanging heavy between his legs.

"Talk to me," he said, lightly grasping Jesse's cock. He lifted it up and out of his way, exposing Jess' smooth sac to his tongue. "I want to know what you want me to do to you. I want to hear the dark secrets that you jerk off to in the middle of the night, what you want more than anything but were always afraid to ask for."

"I like to be bound, helpless. I can't tell you the number of times I thought about you tying me, chaining me, like you did last week." Jess paused for so long that Gideon was about to prompt him for more. "I always used to think about being tied to your bed, completely immobile, stretched spread-eagle. Your fangs are descended. I used to read the old reports about you, about what you used to do to your victims. There were some that survived, some you didn't want to kill. And I always wondered why they were the lucky ones. One day, it occurred to me that maybe the people who wrote the reports couldn't tell the difference between your victims and people who were like me. But I thought I could tell the difference."

Jesse's voice was low and haunting, and the images he evoked made dark coils slither around Gideon's spine. "You're not a victim," Gideon murmured. He sucked one of Jesse's balls into his mouth, relishing how silken the skin was against his lips, and groaned at how delicious it felt. Jesse's fingers tightened in his wet hair, but Gideon pulled off, albeit reluctantly. "Victims don't get the chance to choose." Before Jess replied, he pulled the other ball between his teeth.

Jesse moaned softly. "I know. I thought about you long before I met you, Gideon. I thought about your fangs, and your cock, and your skill with whips, knives, chains, leather…I want you to use my body like it's yours. My skin, my blood, my flesh, I want it all to be yours."

The needy growl rumbled unbidden through Gideon, and he raked his blunt teeth up the length of the cock to suck the dripping head hard into his mouth. Jesse's hands flew to his shoulders, nails digging into the muscle as he swayed against Gideon, but Gideon pried them away, bringing them up to either side of Gideon's face instead. Holding

Jesse's cock steady at the base, he pulled off and looked up to meet Jess' questioning eyes.

"Do I have to order you to fuck my mouth?" he teased.

Jesse's eyes widened, as though such a thing had never occurred to him, and would never occur to him if he had a hundred years to contemplate everything Gideon could do while on his knees. The pressure increased on Gideon's face as Jesse's nails curled into his cheeks, and he allowed himself to be guided back to Jesse's cock. He parted his lips, and Jesse thrust forward immediately with surprising force.

It was not the rhythm Gideon expected, but Jesse's hunger was a shot of adrenaline through his veins. His tongue swirled around the smooth shaft, absorbing the heat, and when Jess pulled back, Gideon let his teeth catch the edges of the crown before skipping over to slide across the head. The effect made Jess drive back in, and quickly, they set a tempo of almost frantic strokes, deeper each time, until Jess finally buried his cock in Gideon's throat.

Gideon sighed in satisfaction, his hands going around to gently cup Jesse's ass in order to hold him in place. He wanted this moment, one where he could both give a little something back to Jess and savor the taste and fullness of him, to last.

Jesse stood perfectly still, but his entire body quivered. His gasps had turned to short, sharp moans, and Gideon realized Jess would stand there for as long as Gideon held him in place, simply waiting. Gideon loosened his grip, and Jesse immediately began moving again, slamming down Gideon's throat. Gideon's throat constricted around his cock, and he looked up, meeting Jesse's gaze. Jess made a shocked, strangled sound and then his warm come filled Gideon's throat.

"Gideon, please bite me…please…I want to feel you…"

Whatever Jess wanted, Gideon knew he couldn't fully give it to him. Gideon had fed from him twice already that night, the second far more filling than it had needed to be. But his begging warmed him even more than the come sliding into his belly. It was impossible to resist, even if Gideon wanted to.

The second he felt Jesse's cock stop twitching, Gideon slid his mouth off, holding the length out of his way as he licked a path to Jess' inner thigh. The artery was easy to find. It pulsed with the force of Jesse's orgasm, and when he felt it throb against his lips, he let his fangs descend and sank them into the yielding flesh.

Jesse slammed his hand against the wall and shouted as loud as his sore throat would let him.

His rich, hot blood filled Gideon's mouth, coated his tongue, and flowed like syrup down his throat. Gideon only took one swallow, though it was very difficult to pull away from the freely flowing blood. He licked Jesse's thigh until the bleeding stopped, and light pink rivulets flowed down Jesse's thighs and across the shower floor.

"I...I think I need to lay down," Jesse said haltingly.

Gideon rose to his feet, curling his arm around Jesse's waist in order to help him stay up. "One thing you're going to have to learn is your blood loss limits," he murmured. With his free hand, he reached behind Jess and turned off the water. "I won't take more than you can give, but do you know how hard it is to keep my head when you beg me like that? It's like the finest music, and all I can think about is giving you what you want."

Jesse smiled thinly. "I'll keep that in mind. I know I probably lost too much already, but I just needed...well, I probably don't need to explain it to you."

Sliding open the doors, Gideon grabbed the nearest towel and dragged it in, drying Jess off. "I made tea. It's probably cold."

"I can reheat it," Jess murmured. "Though at this point, I just want something wet."

Gideon couldn't resist nudging his erection against Jesse's hips. "You know...that could still be arranged. Stretch across the bed, just kind of let your head hang over the edge." He smirked. "I'll do all the work."

"Maybe after the tea."

The smirk turned into a genuine smile, and Gideon tightened his hold around Jesse's waist. "Come on. Let's get you to bed."

CHAPTER 9

Jesse became aware of the world around him long before he opened his eyes. Gideon wasn't in the room, but he heard him in the kitchen, and then heard him running upstairs, rustling around in the office above Jesse's head. Jesse knew they had work to do, but he was in no hurry to jump out of Gideon's bed.

If only because there was a possibility that if he lingered long enough, Gideon would come in for him.

He swallowed, trying to wet his dry, slightly bruised throat, and carefully rolled onto his back. He didn't mind waking up sore. He especially didn't mind waking up sore in Gideon's bed. Images from the night before bombarded him, but the only thing that seemed real was the emotions that very nearly carried him away. The blow jobs, the fucking, the biting, the almost endless come, all of that was already fading. But the insane impulse to tell Gideon over and over and over how much he loved him was still very vivid.

But he couldn't imagine that Gideon would want to hear those words. Jesse was not intimately familiar with Gideon's history—how could he be? Gideon had a lot of it, and if there was one thing Gideon was not into, it was sharing. But he knew enough from his own research, and from the clues Gideon had dropped, to piece together the story.

There was a girl. One Jesse had never met. One who died ten years before Jesse was born. But what was forty years to a creature that was nearly four centuries old? It was nothing. More than once, he had cursed the ghost of a woman he'd never known. All he knew about her was her name—Mary—and that she had been a natural force Gideon couldn't resist. But Jesse shouldn't curse her. Because while she was the reason Gideon was emotionally inaccessible, she was also the reason Gideon was trying to save the very humans he used to prey on.

She was the reason Jesse was working in Gideon's office at all.

Jesse wished he knew more details about their story. How had a vampire with a reputation like Gideon's met and fallen in love with a young black woman during the height of the Civil Rights movement? How had she convinced him he would be better, happier, stopping the monsters that stalked the streets? Had it been the strength of her goodness?

Jesse didn't know and didn't dare ask. All he knew was that Gideon didn't want anything to do with love, and he especially didn't want to fall in love with another fragile human.

That was why Jess wasn't truly angry about Gideon's behavior the night before. He already considered humans pretty far below him in the grand scheme of things. That was natural, since humans had been food for so long, and he was stronger, faster, and in many cases, smarter. But Jesse had thought they really were friends and partners, and Gideon's decision had angered him, but most of all, it had hurt. And when Gideon had said taking him to Sangre at all was a big mistake, he had been teetering on the edge of devastated. Which might have been the only reason he'd had the courage to issue the ultimatum.

Jess opened his eyes. If he had wanted to be Gideon's sex slave with nothing better to do but laze about in bed all day and wait for Gideon to call for him, he wouldn't have bothered with being angry or issuing an ultimatum. But he had.

With a hint of regret at leaving the large, soft bed, Jesse rolled off the mattress, pushing himself to his feet and swaying for a moment. After a few experimental steps, he decided he'd be able to function normally. He smiled and headed for the bathroom, his grin only fading when he remembered he didn't have any clean clothes at Gideon's place.

It returned again when he saw the pile of folded items on the closed toilet lid. An index card had been propped on top, and Jess picked it up to read it, his smile broadening.

> *You didn't really think all I bought were the clothes you wore last night, did you?—G*

He started to set the note down to look at the clothes more closely when he noticed writing on its other side.

Come up to the office when you're dressed. We need to figure out how to move next on the Richards' case.

That, more than the new jeans or shirt, made his smile warm.

Jesse dressed quickly, pausing only for a moment to check his reflection. His neck was still red and raw from the leather collar, and of course, Gideon's mark was still prominent. He couldn't see the one on the back of his neck, but he brushed his fingers over the sensitive skin, sending a chill down his spine to his cock. But the knowledge that Gideon shouldn't really bite him again for at least another day or two cooled his heated blood.

He hurried upstairs, bypassing his own cluttered desk for Gideon's office.

Gideon stood in front of the map of the city he had pinned to the opposite wall. His back was to the door, but Jess knew from the stretch of his thin sweater over his broad shoulders that he had his arms folded in front of him while he studied the meandering streets. It was Gideon pose number seventeen. He did a lot of thinking staring at that map.

"Do you think it's significant that Sangre isn't anywhere near the warehouse?" Gideon asked without turning around.

"I think the most likely explanation is that the warehouse was the most convenient one available for Henry's purposes," Jesse said, moving to stand beside him. A red pushpin indicated Sangre's position, a blue one marked the warehouse. "The club's in the middle of an area with a fairly dense vampire population. He might have chosen a warehouse that was still accessible but not standing out like a beacon for every vampire looking for their next fix."

"True." Gideon still looked unconvinced, though he kept musing aloud. It was how they always worked, bandying theories back and forth until they found one that both felt right—for Gideon—and was logical—for Jess. The fact that they were doing this the morning after their fight didn't escape Jesse's attention. "Its effects are too easily achieved to have it that handy. Were you ever able to get the obsidian on the door knob analyzed?"

"Yes. I got the results back yesterday morning. It's psilocybin based. A simple hallucinogen that really shouldn't have any sort of effect on vampires at all. It's easily absorbed through touch, obviously. Whatever is going on, it's not chemically based."

Gideon fell silent for a moment. "I wasn't hallucinating," he finally said. "So that's probably the medium Henry's using for transferal." He glanced at Jess. "The clothes look good, by the way."

"You have a good eye," Jesse returned, though he knew Gideon wasn't actually complimenting the clothes. "So, are you thinking magic, too?"

"Unfortunately."

Jesse frowned, staring at the map like it really did have the answers they needed. From his own knowledge, and Gideon's tone, he knew it'd have to be very dark magic. And there was only one place in the city to fulfill all their dark magic needs. "I think that means we should visit Black John."

"Christ," Gideon muttered. Running his hand over his hair, he turned away from the map and went over to his desk, sitting heavily in his chair. "You're going to make me go with you, aren't you?"

Jesse almost smiled at the thought of making Gideon do anything he didn't want to do. "I think that would be a good idea. It's the respectful thing to do, and God knows we don't need to be on his bad side."

Gideon rolled his eyes. "I'm *already* on his bad side. What you mean is you don't want me to make it even worse."

Personally, Jess thought Gideon was exaggerating. True, the last time they had been forced to deal with the black mage, Gideon had ended up killing the man's assistant, but the circumstances had been beyond their control. Even Black John had admitted nothing else could have been done, but that didn't change the fractious relationship between the two men.

"Well, do you want to make it worse? I'd hate it if I woke up one morning and you had been turned into a toad or something."

"No, you wouldn't. You'd have too much fun trying to kiss me back into a prince."

"I doubt the spell would be so easily broken. I'd probably have to go on some epic quest, or find him a new assistant, or do his laundry for a month or something."

Gideon muttered something under his breath again. "What if I offer to tie you to the bed and ravish you all day? Will that get me out of going?"

Jesse smiled and perched on the edge of the desk, his knees brushing against Gideon's. "Yes, it would get you out of it, but only because I'd completely forget that I ever intended to leave your bed. Then neither one of us would talk to him, and the investigation will stall."

"Hate to break it to you, Jess, but the investigation's already stalled." Gideon swiveled in his chair, moving so that his hand was within touching distance of Jesse's leg. "Fine. You win. But you're making it up to me later. Us fucking now has gotta have *some* perks."

"Of course," Jess agreed. "But you know, figuring out the make-up of obsidian is really only a small part of what we need to do. Are you going to try to find Tricia tonight?"

"I need to. My gut is telling me she was the last person to see him alive." He paused, his fingers tracing idle patterns on Jesse's leg. In spite of his sore muscles, it was impossible not to feel his cock twitch. "I want to go out alone, Jess. You can stay here and decipher whatever we get from Black John, or go over the coroner's report again to see if there's some clue we're missing, or some other brilliant idea you come up with that'll help this case. But I'm not taking you with me tonight."

"Fair enough," Jesse said, and he meant it. He had hardly been Gideon's shadow before; he didn't need to follow him like a puppy now. "Any specific reason why, or just a general feeling of danger?"

"I need to go back to Sangre. Henry's dealing from there, and Tricia was working with him. *Somebody* is going to know something."

"Oh." The mention of the club prompted mixed feelings, and Jesse didn't mind that he was going to be excluded from that particular outing. "Are we ever going back there…together?"

A sly gleam appeared in Gideon's eyes, and his hand slid higher up Jesse's thigh. "Well, you *better* not go back there without me."

"Well, if I did, I certainly wouldn't want for attention."

"And you wouldn't get out alive."

"You don't think any of them would be so enthralled with me they'd want to keep me as a pet?"

His grip tightened, and Jesse could've sworn he heard Gideon growl. "They better not."

Jesse's lips twitched into a smile. "Or you'll kill them. I remember. You didn't answer my question."

Slipping his hand beneath Jesse's leg, Gideon pulled him off the desk and across his lap, rubbing his groin against Jesse's. It was awkward and uncomfortable, and Jess felt like his legs were a mile long sticking over the side of the chair, but the curl of Gideon's fingers around his nape followed by the deliberate swipe of his tongue over

Jesse's mouth was enough for him not to care.

"I think I'm going to keep you to myself for a little while," Gideon murmured. "We'll get back to Sangre soon enough, but for now…" His tongue probed past Jesse's lips, demanding an instant response.

That was more than fine with Jesse, and he let Gideon know by the way he responded to the kiss. Why did it feel like it had been a small eternity since they'd last touched, last kissed? Gideon stiffened against his groin as the kiss deepened, Jesse's tongue scraping against the blunt points of Gideon's teeth. Gideon growled softly, and Jess knew he was already tasting his blood. Gideon tried to pull him closer, as if there was any room between them, and his fingers tightened on Jesse's nape.

Despite that, Jess managed to break the kiss. "Nice try," he murmured, taking a deep breath. "But you're still coming with me to John's."

Gideon scowled, automatically loosening his hold, allowing Jess to sit up. "Damn."

Jesse stood with great effort—Gideon's lap was not a bad place to be. "I already promised I'd make it up to you."

"Oh, you will." Gideon rose as well, grabbing his car keys as he walked past Jess for the door. "And I'm pretty sure there's going to be clamps involved."

"Are there any other errands we have to run that you need to be bribed into?" Jesse asked, following him out. "I have the feeling now is the time to do it."

Gideon whirled as they reached the stairs and grabbed Jesse's ass, pulling their bodies flush so that their hard cocks rubbed against each other. "No reason to cram everything in to one time," he said, his mouth wet against Jesse's ear. "You've got nights and nights ahead of you to find out everything I've got in the playroom."

"And days, too, I hope," Jesse murmured.

"And you plan on working when?"

"Well, I'm going to need a break occasionally."

Gideon's teeth caught his ear, and then he was breaking away again. Jess had to fight not to drag him back.

"Breaks aren't supposed to last for hours," Gideon said. "Now let's get this over with."

*   *   *

Black John didn't have a storefront. Even in Chicago where there was a vampire on every street corner, a placard announcing "All Your Black Magic Needs in One Convenient Location!" didn't exactly put the local populace at ease. For Black John, that meant working out of his house, which in fact, made him even more powerful. It put him at the center of very deep, very elemental magic, and even if he had to concede some of that by inviting Gideon into his home, it was still potent enough to knock half the city on its ass.

Gideon didn't like one man having so much power at his disposal. Black John had no patience for people who played both sides against the other, like he thought Gideon did. It was a hate/hate relationship that worked for them.

That didn't mean racing through the pouring rain to the man's front door didn't make Gideon itch in the worst possible way. Even with Jess at his side—who John adored—he felt like he was walking into the lion's den. One of these days, John was going to tear Gideon to pieces, he just knew it.

"Last chance for hours of mind-blowing sex from a very grateful vampire who'll tie you to his bed and make you forget your own name," Gideon offered, shaking the rain from his hair.

"I'll settle for hours of mind-blowing sex from a very annoyed vampire who'll tie me to his bed and make me forget my own name," Jesse countered, ringing the bell.

"I gotta live through this first," Gideon muttered.

He kept a half-step behind Jess as footsteps approached the other side of the door. Better to have Jesse's be the first face John saw. They'd have better luck that way.

Out of the corner of his eye, he saw the curtain flicker at the window he stood next to. Damn it. So much for trying to garner good will.

The door opened and John stood in the narrow space, looking up to both men. Though diminutive in height, with an unlined face and clear gray eyes that could have been fifteen or fifty, there was nothing unassuming about Black John. There was a precision to how he held himself, and the way his eyes darted so quickly from one object to another gave the distinct impression that he was about to strike, even if he hadn't moved a muscle elsewhere. It was worse for anyone with heightened senses. He reeked of magic. The entire effect was that you were watching Andy Hardy after he'd graduated from the Charles Manson Charm School.

"Since I know Gideon would rather get soaked to the skin than seek shelter from a storm under my roof, one can only assume you need my help with something," John said smoothly. His gaze settled on Jess, and though a slight smile curved his mouth, his voice was tinged with disappointment. "Once upon a time, you would have called rather than show up unannounced on my doorstep, Mr. Madding. You've been with your employer too long. His bad manners are starting to rub off on you."

Jesse inclined his head slightly, a sign of respect that irritated Gideon. "You're right, of course, I apologize. I hope this excuses my rudeness," he said, pushing a small box into John's hand. "We wouldn't have come if wasn't an emergency."

John lifted the lid, tilting his head slightly to peer inside. He lifted a single brow. "Where did you find this? I heard they were all destroyed."

This was a petrified kimura-gumo Gideon had received as payment on a recent case. The Japanese spider had been one of thirteen that had been part of an attempted resurrection he'd interrupted at a gaming convention downtown, the lone survivor when he'd torched the place. He'd argued with Jess about the wisdom in giving a powerful talisman to the blackest mage in town, but in the end, he'd lost. From John's reaction, Gideon was wishing he'd fought a little harder.

Opening the door wider, John stepped back, allowing them room to enter. "Emergencies are always the most fun," he said. He didn't even look at Gideon. "Come in, gentlemen."

Jesse glanced over his shoulder to Gideon before he crossed his threshold. *Please behave, we won't be here long.* Gideon nodded and followed him inside. Jess pulled another object out of his pocket, carefully wrapped in a thick towel. As he held it out to John, Gideon realized it was the knob from the warehouse.

"I found a substance coated on this. We believe it's a drug popular with vampires, known as obsidian. I ran an analysis on it and discovered it's nothing more than mushrooms. In other words, chemistry can't explain the effect it has on vamps."

"Because Nietzsche had it all wrong." John didn't open the towel to look at the knob before handing it back. "Better living doesn't happen through chemistry. It's all about power."

"What sort of power and where is it coming from?" Jesse asked.

"Why do you care? It's for vampires, not..." He finally looked at Gideon, and a shrewd glint appeared in his eye. Gideon balled his hands in his pockets to keep from giving the man the satisfaction of a visible reaction. "I missed it. Damn."

"I *care* because this has already caused at least one very violent, very public death. If there are many more like that, it'll plunge the city into chaos." Jesse stepped to the side, blocking John's view of Gideon. "John, you know it's a very precarious balance between relative peace and open warfare."

"And I fail to see why this qualifies as an emergency. We live in a fragile ecosystem, Mr. Madding, and yet it manages to continue regardless. All I've done is help a few vampires rediscover their true natures. Life goes on."

Jesse blinked. "So this *is* your work? Why would you do this?"

"I took a job that paid me very well. Isn't that why we all do what we do?"

"No. No, my job pays me shit. No offense, Gideon." Gideon waved him off. "Who signed the check, John?"

"Payment isn't always about money," John said with a small smile.

"Did he buy your loyalty as well, John? How much is your integrity on sale for?"

John's smile faded, and his eyes darkened. A crackle of magic in the air made the hair on the back of Gideon's neck stand on end, and he stepped forward to Jesse's side, muscles poised to block anything John might throw at him.

"I would suggest purchasing a mirror," John said softly, "but considering your choice of associates, I'm pretty sure it would be pointless. There's no reason for slander. I sold the elixir you're interested in to Henry Echols. But then again, I'm sure you already knew that."

Despite Gideon's tension, Jesse seemed calm. "What's your asking price for the elixir?"

Gideon's attention snapped away from John to Jess. "Are you nuts? You're not bringing that stuff back to the office."

"I'm not going to let you play with it, Gideon," Jesse said calmly, his eyes still on John. "I'll put it in a safe place."

"Yeah, because that worked so well the first time."

Jess sent him an exasperated glance. "We'll be more careful this time, okay?"

With a put-upon sigh, John turned on his heel and headed down the hall. "Save the Abbott and Costello routine, gentlemen. Just give me a moment. I'll be right back with what you want."

When John disappeared through a doorway, Gideon frowned. "He's not giving us the elixir for free, is he?"

"No, he'll probably ask for my soul." Gideon's eyebrows knitted more tightly together and Jesse touched his elbow. "I'm kidding. He won't ask for payment now, but he'll expect something later."

"Great," Gideon muttered. "But just so you know, I'm reserving the right to say I told you so when we're both burning in hell."

John's return prevented Jess from making more inappropriate jokes, but Gideon refused to retreat as John approached. He held out a clear jam jar, filled a third full with a black, viscous fluid, to Jess.

"That's all I currently have. Henry's order was…quite large."

"Can this be diluted and still remain effective?"

John walked past them to open the front door. "What's the point of only unlocking a cage if you don't intend to let out the beast that resides within?" His unwavering gaze fixed on them, waiting for them to leave. "Good day, gentlemen."

"A good day to you, too," Jesse said, almost sounding pleasant. He gripped the jar carefully and led the way out the door.

His calm demeanor didn't crack until they were safely outside, and then the anger that he had only allowed a glimpse of earlier lit up his face. "I know I shouldn't feel betrayed by the stunt he pulled, but I really do." He marched over to Gideon's car, every line of his body tense. "Honestly, what was that bullshit?"

Now wasn't the time for reminding Jess that he hadn't wanted to come to John's in the first place, Gideon decided. Rarely did Jess get this angry.

"The reason we do what we do," he said instead. "The important thing is, we've got confirmation that it's Henry. I'll definitely be hitting up Sangre tonight."

"I don't want you to go alone." He held up a hand. "I know, I'm not going. You've made that clear. Hell, I wish you weren't going at all. It'll be too easy for you to come in contact with that crap."

Gideon turned the key in the ignition, mulling over the possibilities. "I'm not sure I trust anybody else enough to bring in on this," he said. When Jess opened his mouth to argue, he shook his head. "I'll be careful. I promise. The last thing I want is to lose control."

Jesse's lips thinned. "I guess John's motivation is pretty clear, but what's Henry's? Is it just money? There are far less dangerous and more potent drugs out there for demons and vampires, if he just wants to turn a profit. Why go to John and request something that will—how did he put it?—unlock the cage and let out the beast within."

"I don't know," Gideon admitted. "But that's what I'm going to find out."

CHAPTER 10

The drive back to the office was tense. Gideon knew Jess was in knots over his misplaced trust in John, but he couldn't get his thoughts away from the inky fluid sloshing around in the jar Jess so carefully cradled. He kept glancing at it out of the corner of his eye, watching it cling to the smooth glass before dripping back down to pool in the bottom, remembering what it had felt like seeping into his skin. Like fire being set to his veins. It was more potent than drinking blood or feeling a heart falter on his tongue.

He would never admit it aloud, not to Jess, not to anybody, but Gideon had reveled in the liberation of those few hours when he'd been high on the obsidian. It was freedom not to care about the restraints society—both human and vampire—placed on him. The only thing Gideon didn't like was not being able to predict his own behavior. Being out of control was his less than preferred mindset.

He didn't turn off the engine when he pulled into his parking spot. "I'm going to head on out," he said before Jesse's curious glance could be vocalized into a query. He tried not to look at the obsidian. "Sangre won't open for hours yet, but I'm going to see if I can shake down some old sources. See what the word is on the street about this shit. I'll keep you updated."

Jess, as astute as ever, nodded as he curled his hands around the jar, hiding its contents as best he could. "I'll try and determine what's in the elixir." He paused. "I might need to go to Michelle's for a text to help me."

Mention of the bookstore owner only worsened Gideon's mood, but he dismissed it. "Get whatever it takes."

His knuckles were white around the steering wheel as Jess got out of the car. It took his friend's calm voice to drag his gaze away from the windshield.

"Be careful," Jess said softly.

Gideon nodded. These days, it felt like his whole life was careful.

The rain was incessant as he trawled the Chicago streets. Black storm clouds blocked out any hint of dangerous sunlight, but the roiling weather matched Gideon's bleak mood. Things didn't improve when his first three stops left him banging on unanswered doors. Either nobody was home, or nobody wanted to see him. Gideon was getting pretty sick and tired of feeling like the odd man out in town.

His fourth at least opened the door to him.

Dull, yellow eyes looked up at him through too-thick mascara. "Fuck," Rina muttered. Her stick-thin arm blocked the entrance, but they both knew she was no match for Gideon physically. It didn't stop the female vampire from trying. She was all spit and vinegar, and in spite of her predilection for getting high with teenagers, Gideon rather liked her. She'd been turned and then abandoned by her sire, but after a run-in with Gideon at a bar around the corner from his office when she created a rumpus after being refused entry, she'd taken the advice he'd given her about how to exist in Chicago without getting killed and run with it. Six years later, she was still around. Not once in that time period had she given him a reason to kill her. That took balls. Gideon respected that.

"It wasn't me," she said before he could greet her. "And if that asshole told you it was, he's fucking lying."

Gideon leaned against the jamb. "Maybe you should tell me your side of the story then," he said. If he played along like he knew what she was talking about, she'd be more likely to cooperate after he let her off on whatever misdemeanor she was afraid of being blamed for.

Rina pushed a lank strand of dishwater blonde hair out of her eyes. "I did exactly like he told me. I took the shit downtown, I put it in the box, I left. Somebody else stole it. You think I'm so dumb I'd be trying to rip off Henry of all people?"

He didn't react on the outside, but Gideon's stomach lurched. It was not the name he had expected, though Henry was the reason he'd sought Rina out in the first place. She used him to buy drugs for the kids she hung out with; Gideon had figured she might have something to say about obsidian or even Tricia.

"If you didn't take it, then, who did?"

"How the fuck should I know? You know how many vampires are crawling through this town. It could be any one of them."

Gideon frowned. "Blaming the entire city doesn't exactly help you sound innocent, Rina."

With an exasperated sigh, Rina released her grip on the jamb and flounced back into her dingy apartment. Gideon followed her in, trying not to show his disdain for the wall-to-wall trash or the rats he heard scuttling behind the walls.

"I know it's not your bag, Gideon, but have you ever *seen* someone hopped up on obsidian? Don't tell me they wouldn't steal it if they saw the opportunity. *Especially* if they're already hopped up. I don't care what fucking line Henry tried to sell you, but I did my job. I made the drop. It's his problem if his buyer didn't get it, not mine."

It wasn't Gideon's problem, either, but what the story told him painted the obsidian picture even blacker. Henry was spreading the drug around more widely, and worse, it was so badly wanted that vamps were stealing it in order to get their hands on it. The chaos he and Jess feared was already encroaching, and if they didn't do something soon, the entire city was going to collapse.

"I'll make you a deal," he said. "I'll convince Henry to get off your case if you help me find one of Henry's girls."

Rina flopped down onto her beat-up couch, her features shifting back to her plain Jane looks. She looked even younger in her human mask. "Since when do you care about one of his skanks? I've seen some of the people you hook up with at Sangre. You can do way better than anybody who'd have anything to do with Henry."

He ignored her commentary. "Do we have a deal or not?"

"Who're you looking for?"

"Tricia."

He knew the instant he said the name that she knew who he was talking about. And he decided in that second that there was no way he was leaving without getting the information he wanted. He didn't want to beat it out of Rina, but he would. In the end, the life of one druggie vamp couldn't compare to the peace of an entire city.

"All I gotta do is tell you where you can find her?"

Maybe he wouldn't have to resort to violence after all.

"That's all you have to do, Rina."

She grinned. It almost made her look innocent. "Deal."

*　　　*　　　*

"What the hell happened to you?"

Jesse stopped short, his hand poised to grab a book off the top shelf. He looked to the source of the question from the corner of his eye. "Nothing?"

Michelle narrowed her eyes. "Right, nothing. That's why you look like shit and you winced reaching for that book. Did you get in a fight?"

"It happens in my line of work," Jesse said mildly, his fingers closing around an old, leather spine. He had hoped to get in and out of the book store without seeing Michelle, but those hopes had been slim. She was always there, even though she insisted that she slept and ate elsewhere.

She stepped behind him, rudely pulling his collar down to look at the nape of his neck. "What? Was there an all-you-can-eat Jesse buffet?"

"No," he said, ducking away from her and straightening his shirt. "How much is this book?"

"I'm not selling that book to you."

Jesse frowned. "Why not?"

"Because you're lying to me, and I don't sell my books to liars," she announced, spinning on her heel. "Put that back where you found it."

"I need this book."

"I need a million dollars."

"It's a matter of life and death."

"Whose?"

"A lot of innocent people."

Michelle waved her hand. "There are no innocent people in this world."

"There are people who don't deserve to die the way Toby Richards did."

She eyed him over her glasses. "Are you saying there are people in this world who do deserve to die that way?" She sniffed. "Oh, wait, look who I'm talking to."

"Michelle, that's not fair."

"So, what did you do to deserve that?" she asked, gesturing at his neck.

"What's with the third degree? You've never minded taking Gideon's money before."

"Gideon never bit a hunk out of your neck before."

Jesse set the book on the counter, but he kept his hand on it so she couldn't snatch it away from him. He liked Michelle, but she had a long-standing grudge against Gideon that Jess couldn't explain. Of course, he realized Gideon rubbed a lot of people the wrong way, and everybody who hated him probably had a good reason to.

"We're trying to figure out who killed Toby Richards. There's nothing we can do about him, but we have reason to suspect a powerful drug was involved. One that could wreak havoc if it ever gets widely disseminated."

"What does that have to do with your neck?"

More than you know. But if Jesse tried to explain how the drug had affected Gideon, Michelle would have led the angry mob to his door. He didn't know her age, but he doubted she was more than fifty. And she was built to fight. She had a body as impassive as a brick wall, and a face to match. She seemed to get thicker and meaner with each passing year, and she wasn't afraid of a fight, fair or not. Jesse loved her dearly, but only when her impatience and anger weren't directed at him.

"It could infect Gideon, and every other vampire in the city. It makes them…"

"Nearly kill their associates?"

"It removes whatever control they have. You know a lot of vampires are trying to live in the human world, or at least, trying to coexist in the city without attracting attention. Can you imagine what a drug like this can do?"

"Why won't you answer my questions?"

"Why won't you listen to me?"

Michelle regarded him with cobalt eyes. "Jesse, you're a good boy. I like seeing you around. I like the books you bring me, and I like the way you always treat the books you buy. And I can ignore who you've aligned yourself with. I don't like it, but you're a big boy, and I guess I can't do anything about it. But you're crossing lines you can't even see."

Jesse listened to her small speech calmly. He wasn't surprised. Humans who fraternized with vampires were about as popular around town as Gideon. And Michelle never bothered to hide her true feelings anyway. "What do you want to know?"

"Are you in danger?"

"No."

"Come here, I want to show you something," she said, turning to the door. She didn't check to see if Jesse was following her as she disappeared behind a curtain that hid a steep, narrow staircase.

He followed her downstairs. The narrow building had a basement and a sub-basement. Jesse knew about the rooms, but she never invited him downstairs, which only fed his secret suspicions that she actually lived in the store.

But the basement didn't boast a small apartment. There were more bookshelves. Several fans were running to keep the room dry, and the bulbs in the low hanging light fixtures were very dim. Each book on the shelf was housed in a sealed plastic bag, and she handed him a pair of latex clubs as he entered the room.

"This is where I keep my rare books."

Jesse nodded mutely. It was like stepping into the inner-sanctum of an ancient temple—a great surprise and an even greater honor. "This is...amazing."

"It is."

"Do you have more downstairs?"

"Yes, but nothing you need to see."

Jesse would have disagreed. "But there's something I need to see down here?"

"When did you first learn about vampires?"

Jesse frowned. "I don't know. I was probably eight or nine. I got into my father's library and I thought all the old sketches and photographs were fake, like the pictures of fairies my mum kept in her sun room."

"But they weren't."

"No, of course not."

"And when did you learn of Gideon?"

Jesse smiled slightly. That particular memory wasn't in danger of fading. "I was fifteen. Father had finally allowed me to start investigating his books, and there was a picture of Gideon from the 1920s."

"Here in Chicago?"

He shrugged. "I guess so. Hasn't Gideon been here since around the turn of the century?"

She went directly to a book on the middle shelf. One of many bound in brown leather that looked entirely innocuous. He couldn't see the title in the dim light as Michelle carefully pulled it out of the bag. Slowly, almost reverently, she opened the book and turned the pages unerringly. She silently handed him the open book.

It was a picture of Gideon that he had never seen before. His smile was full of fangs, but oddly playful. He was standing in the middle of two women and two men, and Jesse was almost certain that the other four in the photo were humans. Humans who looked startlingly young, but their eyes seemed very old. Jesse didn't know if that was a trick of the light. Gideon had a possessive hand around the nearest woman's waist, and his other hand was blocked by one of the men—who wasn't much more than a boy. Jesse thought he knew what Gideon was doing with his hand.

"It's a good likeness of him."

Michelle turned the page, and there was another photograph of the five of them, but now they were mostly naked. Their poses were still stiff and proper, but their smiles were more playful, their skin pale. She kept turning the page, revealing photo after photo. Soon they were all completely naked. And then the poses changed.

Gideon with his cock in a girl's mouth. Gideon with his mouth wrapped around somebody else's cock. Gideon fucking the other girl. Gideon with his head buried between the same girl's thighs—possibly sucking his own come from her pussy. One picture featured Gideon and the young man with dark hair. He was bent over at the waist, touching his toes, and Gideon was gripping his hips, the tip of his cock already buried in the man's ass.

The final photo looked to be a blood bath.

"Why are you showing me these? Do you think I forgot he was a vampire?"

"Do you think these kids thought they were going to die? When they dressed in their finest clothes to pose with Gideon, do you think they knew they were wearing their funeral shrouds?"

"Gideon is different now."

"Gideon is a vampire. They don't change. They can't. There are so many photographs like this. I know the ones I have here barely touch the tip of the iceberg and I have at least another dozen picture books."

"Where did you get these?"

She shrugged. "Various collectors. It doesn't matter. What makes you think you're different from these kids? From any of these kids?"

"If he planned to kill me, he would have done so by now."

Michelle yanked the book from him with more force than she should have. "That's your answer? You must be safe because he hasn't bathed in your blood yet?"

"He's my friend, Michelle."

"Do you think he has the same concept of friendship that you do?"

"Do you think I'd still be alive now if he didn't, Michelle? He didn't have to hire me, give me a job and a place to stay until I was back on my feet again. In the nearly forty years since he started Gideon Investigations, he always worked alone. He didn't even know me at first. But I proved to him that I could be useful, and that's all he ever asked from me."

She looked at his neck. "That's all?"

"I've been in some tight spots, and in the two years I've known Gideon, he's never left me in those spots by myself."

"I think you're making a mistake."

"So noted, but it doesn't change anything."

"I had to try, Jesse. I hope you understand." She held the book out to him. "Take this. I think you need to have a reminder of how things could go."

Jesse took it with a small nod. "I appreciate the gift."

"I'll sell you the other book you wanted."

Jesse smiled. "I thought you probably would."

"Just promise me you won't let him go too far," Michelle said, taking his elbow and leading him back to the stairs.

"Believe it or not, I don't actually have a death wish. I won't let him go too far."

"That doesn't actually make me feel better," she muttered.

"So, are you going to let me come down here again?"

"No."

"Please?"

"Absolutely not."

"Why not?"

"It's my porn collection, Jess. I don't expect you to let me root around under your bed, do I? Well, I guess these days, it's probably all on your computer."

Jesse laughed as they stepped into the brightly lit store. "The bottom of my closet, actually."

"You owe me eighty dollars for that book."

Jesse grimaced. "Put it on my tab?"

"You better pay up before you try to take any more books out of this store. I'm not running a charity here."

He promised to do just that as she carefully wrapped the book and slid it into a paper bag. His mind was still reeling from the day's events, but as he hurried through the thick heat of the late evening, all he could think about were those damned photos.

*   *   *

Gideon would never have found her in a million years. The vampires of Chicago were—most of the time—creatures of habit. They lived in the same areas, chose the same neighborhoods for kills, hung out at the same demon-safe venues. They rarely broke from these patterns, and all Gideon thought as he stood outside the greenhouse was that Tricia was one gutsy demon. There would be few options for hiding when the sun was out. Nobody would ever think to find her here.

It was easy to break in, not so easy to figure out where to start first. The greenhouse was huge, and felt even larger with the echo of the rain on the glass roof resounding between its walls. Gideon picked up one of the directory brochures and thumbed through it, ignoring the layout of the plants in favor of locating the security offices. Tricia might not have a reflection, but modern technology was a bit more sophisticated than mirrors these days.

More importantly, Gideon was not a stupid vampire.

He found her almost immediately, though he recognized it was more luck than any type of skill. Using his map, he plotted a route to Rare Flowers and crept through the silent rows, eyes glittering gold as he scanned for any sign of movement. The dearth of sound would have been eerie to anyone not accustomed to it, but Gideon was a predator, had been for centuries. A vampire who didn't even have the sense not to get on the wrong side of one of the most powerful humans in Chicago didn't stand a chance.

Gideon slapped his hand over her mouth, dragging her back against the hard wall of his body. Her fangs descended, trying to slash through the tough skin of his palm, but he merely tightened his hold, waiting her out until her struggles stopped.

"Like to slaughter your boyfriends, do you?" he growled in her ear. "Good thing for me I have no interest in being your friend."

CHAPTER 11

Jesse was reasonably certain the office was still empty when he returned, but he still searched through both the office and the apartment looking for any sign of Gideon. He wanted to study the photographs closer, but he didn't necessarily want Gideon to know he had them. Not yet.

Jess settled on the couch in Gideon's apartment, turning on every light in the room to study the tiny print that accompanied each picture. He hoped it would supply more clues about the victims' identities, as well as the context of the photos. Who was behind the camera? Another vampire? A human? Did the photographer survive long after he snapped the final image? Who developed the film? Who took the time to publish it?

He hoped the title page would help answer those questions, but there was no title page, or anything resembling a copyright page. The cover was similarly unmarked. No title, no author, no publisher, nothing one would expect to find on a cover. Jesse realized it had been privately bound. This might have been the only copy in existence. Had Gideon hired, or forced, somebody to make this book for his own private collection? That seemed like the most reasonable guess, but if that was the case, how had Michelle acquired it?

There were prints before he reached the section Michelle had shown him, but none of them featured Gideon, or anybody Jesse recognized from the other photos. Many of them were explicit, staged sex, but others had a more PG-rating. They didn't seem at all the sort of thing

Gideon would want to keep for his own pleasure. His tastes for sex weren't so vanilla, and as far as his tastes for art went, he usually liked work that was more bold, more startling, even disturbing and frightening.

Even though he knew how this particular series of photos would end, he still felt a thrill at the first sight of Gideon. Aesthetically, he was a truly beautiful creature. That judgment was completely separate from Jesse's physical attraction to the vampire. Tall, muscular, with flashing black eyes and that wicked, full mouth. He would challenge anybody to look at Gideon, without any preconceptions, and admit he wasn't stunning.

The text beneath the first photograph provided names and identities. The girl with the black hair was Anna, and the girl closest to Gideon was called Maggie. The boy closest to Gideon was Sam, and the fourth member of the party was identified as George. Nobody had last names or ages. They looked younger than ever to Jesse in the bright light, though he didn't place them much below eighteen.

Jesse flipped through the pages slowly, taking his time to study the details of each one. He was forced to unzip his pants when Gideon began appearing fully nude. He felt like he might have been doing something a little wrong—this was not supposed to be wanking material. But Gideon's body had always had a strong effect on him, and the new ability to admire, worship, kiss, and touch that body didn't dampen his immediate reaction to the sight of it. If anything, it made the reaction stronger, quicker.

He turned to the picture that had caught his attention before. He saw now that Sam was the one in the photo, and he was gripping his ankles, the tips of his hair brushing against the ground. Both Sam and Gideon were in profile, and Gideon's cock was stiff, acting like a bridge to link Sam's slim body with Gideon's much broader frame. Gideon was holding his hips, possibly to keep from knocking him over.

It was far too easy to imagine himself in Sam's place. Curious, he went to the next page, and it was the same pose, only Gideon's cock was half into his ass. In the third image, Gideon was fully seated. Jesse took his cock in hand, stroking himself slowly, trying to ease the sudden throbbing, and he immediately realized his own hand wasn't going to be enough.

He was still sore from the night before, but he desperately wanted Gideon's cock. He never took his eyes from the book. Was this the first time Gideon had fucked Sam, or had it been a regular occurrence? Did

Gideon fuck him slowly? Or had it been the more punishing pace that he used with Jesse?

Jess ran his palm over his tip, gathering the thick drops of pre-come and smearing it over the head. He rotated his wrist, circling his cock with his palm, spreading more and more of the clear fluid. He set the book aside, but kept the page open, his other hand moving between his thighs to gently squeeze and pull on his balls.

He reached over, turning the pages back to the one with Gideon sucking George's cock. He focused on George's face. Something like pure bliss colored it, and his eyes were open, focused on Gideon, adoring. Not that Jesse blamed the guy. He probably had a similar look when Gideon got between his legs. He began stroking himself, moving his hand in long, quick jerks.

In the past, most of his fantasies had been reserved for Gideon, but now it was different. Instead of wondering what it would feel like to have his cock buried in Gideon's throat, he could recall every detail, every touch, every bit of pressure and subtle shift of Gideon's tongue. Instead of wondering if Gideon would tie him up, he knew to expect chains and a leash. Instead of imagining just how far Gideon would be willing to go with him, he felt the phantom memory of the whip on his shoulders and back.

He moved his arm faster, shaking the couch with his effort. The pages fell backward, until the final one was staring back at Jess. He'd have to stop to flip the photos back, or close the book entirely, and he didn't want to stop. His thighs tensed, his back straightened, and he looked away from the book at the last moment before he climaxed.

"Last night wasn't enough for you?"

Everything in him jerked at the sound of Gideon's voice, and Jess scrambled to try and tuck himself away as he shifted to see Gideon standing in the doorway. His hair was wet, plastered to his forehead, as was his dark shirt to his muscled chest. There were fresh scratches scored down his cheek, and mud stained the cuffs of his pants. Something had happened. The question was what.

Gideon's eyes flickered to the book lying open at Jesse's side, and his brows drew together slightly. "What are you looking at?"

Jesse wiped his hands on his pants before closing the book. He didn't know what he felt more awkward about. The fact that he had been getting himself off while Gideon was out getting drenched and scratched, or what he was getting himself off to. "It's a book," he said lamely. "Michelle...gave it to me."

"Michelle's dealing in porn now?"

"Not dealing in it, no. But it seems she's got quite the impressive collection in the basement." He stood and held the book out to Gideon. "It's not so much porn as her idea of a warning."

Jess studied Gideon closely, gauging his every reaction. There was the moment of hesitation before Gideon took the text. There was the brush of his thumb over the spine when he tilted it to look for the title. There was the lowering of his lashes as he simply regarded the cover before handing it back, unopened.

"I hope you didn't get anything on the pages," he commented. "It's one of a kind."

"Please, Gideon. You know me better than that." He held the book loosely at his side. "Did you have it made?"

"No. It was never mine. I was just asked to..." He paused, his eyes inscrutable as he searched for the word he wanted. "...contribute."

Jesse nodded. "It was clearly somebody's private volume. Did the other members know what they were contributing to?"

A longer pause. "No. We thought that would spoil the effect."

"Do you think I should take it as the warning she intended?"

For the first time since being noticed, Gideon's façade crumpled a bit. He ran his hand through his hair, pushing the wet strands off his brow, and then rolled his neck, as if to release tension. "What do you want me to say, Jess? You've known all along I have a past. You never seemed to have a problem with it before. Or last night. Or hell, even now." He took a sudden step forward, entering Jesse's personal space and leaning in to sniff at his neck. "Do you have any idea what you smell like? This moment, right after you've come, this is when you smell the most delicious. Because your blood is still hot, and your heart is still racing, and all I want is to tear into your throat and ass until you bleed even more. So you tell me. Is it a warning or not?"

Jesse's mouth ran dry, and even though most of his instincts screamed at him to back off, he took a step closer. "I don't have a problem with your past. I never have. I'm more worried about what you're doing now." He tilted his head, exposing his neck further. "I more or less told Michelle to mind her own business. But I would like to know what the difference for you is between me and them"

He felt the brush of Gideon's nose against his skin the moment before Gideon cupped a hand around the back of his neck and held him utterly still.

"The difference is knowing when to stop and then caring enough to actually do it." When Gideon snaked his tongue around the shell of Jesse's ear, a shiver ran down Jess' spine. "Even when I know how badly you want it."

Jesse clutched Gideon's shirt with one hand, his other hand sneaking between their bodies to cup Gideon's erection. "I'm glad one of us knows when to stop," he murmured. "Because sometimes I do want it."

Gideon snorted. "I'm beginning to wonder if your definition of sometimes is the same as Webster's." Carefully, he folded his hands over Jesse's and peeled them off, pushing him away at the same time. "I came up because I found Tricia. I thought you'd want to know."

Jesse blinked stupidly, his brain still three steps back, fixated on Gideon's mouth so close to his neck. "Tricia? You brought her here?" Saying her name seemed to help. "Are the scratches courtesy of her?

Gideon nodded. "She tried making a dash for it when I was dragging her ass back out to the car. Let's say she's not exactly thrilled about being here."

"No, I can't imagine she would be." Jesse put the book away on a high shelf. "I want to come up and hear what she has to say."

"I don't think that would be a good idea."

Jesse immediately wanted to protest that Gideon couldn't shield him from half of the investigation, but he was tired of that particular song and dance routine. "Gideon, I'm going to need every bit of information I can get to identify the ingredients in the elixir. I doubt you're going to be able to keep track of every tiny, seemingly insignificant detail, but I can."

"You can," Gideon conceded. "But do you *really* want to watch me strip the skin from Tricia to get it? And be honest, Jess. This isn't about sex. This is about watching me use every means in my power to get her to talk, because right now, she's more scared of Henry than me. I have to change her way of thinking."

No, he really didn't. Gideon had always kept him from the interrogations, and Jesse had always been happy not to press the issue. But they had never had a case that frightened him like this. At least one person was dead, but Jesse did not doubt for a second that the body count was much higher than that. *He* would have been dead if Gideon had wanted to kill him more than he wanted to fuck him. And the elixir he had carefully stored away was like a ticking time bomb, silently counting down the seconds to the moment when all their efforts would be made futile.

"I don't want to see it, Gideon. But I don't want to start finding more mutilated and brutalized corpses, either. Getting the information I need is more important than protecting my delicate sensibilities."

A small smile lifted the corner of Gideon's mouth. "Delicate is not a word I would ever use to describe you." He paused. "Promise you won't intervene in any way."

"I'm just going to observe, Gideon, I promise. This is entirely your deal, and I'm happy to keep it that way."

Gideon was nodding before he finished speaking. "All I've been able to get from her so far is that she's been hiding from Henry ever since Toby's death. That's why she hasn't been around Sangre. The question is why."

Jesse thought the answer to that was obvious—fear. They didn't need to look at the why, they needed to worry about the what. What monster scared the monsters? "Let me wash up and get my notebook. I can meet you upstairs."

He watched Gideon turn and leave, and promptly did the same. The soft sound of his name being called out made him stop.

"What's the difference between me now and the me in the book?" Gideon's eyes were dark and solemn, fixed so intently on him that it felt like an embrace. "For you, Jess."

"You want to do good now. I don't believe you would kill four innocent people for the sake of somebody's private...art...collection. I'm not saying that you couldn't, but you wouldn't." Jesse half shrugged. That wasn't the largest difference. The vampire in the book was a face, a body, and an act, but he wasn't the man Jesse had spent the last two years with. "The difference is that you're my friend."

The answer seemed to satisfy Gideon, and he turned again to go upstairs.

"Gideon?" He paused, looking over his shoulder. "Do you mind if I keep the book?"

"Truth? Yeah, I mind. I don't much...like the man in that book. But I trust you meant what you said. So if you want to keep it, I'll deal." A ghost of a smile haunted his face. "Besides, I know how fucking hot most of those pictures are. I can't say I can blame you for wanting to keep 'em around."

"Fair enough. Maybe we'll just have to replace them with our own pictures some time," Jesse suggested as Gideon disappeared upstairs.

Glancing at the book, he smiled wryly. He was sure whatever Michelle intended to happen, it wasn't this sort of discussion and negotiation. But then, she wouldn't have believed a word Gideon said anyway. He did, though. Every single one. Sometimes, that felt like asking for trouble. But now it felt like the right thing to do.

CHAPTER 12

If he'd given Tricia much thought, she would have been exactly as Gideon would have expected someone like Toby Richards to date. She was California pretty, with plush curves and a too-sharp fashion sense. Her long blonde hair was bleached a lighter shade than was natural, and her pale skin was flawless, though now, there were faint bruises on her face where Gideon had held his hand over her mouth. Gideon wasn't sure if even Jess would be able to tell she was a vampire when she wasn't fanged out. She passed *that* well.

At the moment, she glared at him with yellow eyes, her arms stretched over her head from where he had her suspended from the ceiling. The chains he used were heavier duty than he'd used on Jesse to accommodate her superior strength, but Tricia was making few attempts to actually get away. She simply watched him, waiting for him to make the first move.

Jesse was watching as well. It was taking all of Gideon's control not to glance at where Jess sat in the corner. He had the perfect vantage to hear what Tricia might say, but that also put him in the position to see as well. There were reasons why Gideon had always conducted interrogations in private, not the least of which was he didn't wish to add further fodder for nightmares for his best friend. Now, his motivation was more selfish. This showed Gideon at his basest to the man now in his bed. Gideon didn't want what Jess might see to be cause for this new relationship to end before it began.

He blocked out everything but the purpose of his task. He needed information only Tricia could provide. It was time to get it.

Folding his arms over his chest, Gideon stood in front of her and held her gaze until she began squirming underneath it. "This doesn't have to be so hard, you know," he said, almost casually. "All you have to do is answer my questions."

Tricia's eyes hardened, and her words dripped with disdain. "What do you think *you* can do to me?"

He refused to indulge his amusement by responding. Instead, Gideon turned on his heel and walked back to his cupboard, his gaze flickering only once to Jess. Whether Jess was aware of it or not, his heart rate jumped with every step closer Gideon got. There wasn't any arousal, though. Thank God. Gideon wasn't sure he'd be able to go through with this, with Jess in the room, if Jess watched the entire interrogation steeped with desire.

Tricia's eyes widened when Gideon returned to stand in front of her with a long stiletto. She had no time to speak before the knife sliced her sundress from her body. He wasn't surprised that she wore nothing underneath, or that her nipples hardened as soon as they were exposed to the warm air.

"Last chance to do this the easy way," he said.

Her eyes were full of loathing. "Hit me with your best shot."

He shrugged. Nobody ever listened when he offered the easy way.

This time when he came back from the cupboard, Gideon held a stoppered bottle of clear fluid. Sucking some into the pipet, he touched the wet tip to the flesh above her right nipple and squeezed to release it over the hard tip. Immediately, her skin began to sizzle and smoke, and Gideon stepped back to gauge her reaction.

"Gotta love holy water," he commented. "Well, I do, at least."

Tricia writhed in the heavy chains, trying to move away from him, but she couldn't get far. Her gaze flickered over the room and her nostrils flared. "Who's your pet?"

Gideon refrained from glancing back at Jess. "Well, it's good to know that Henry's still picking his girls based on their cup size and not their IQ. I ask you the questions, not the other way around. Who killed Toby Richards?"

"Who?"

He shook his head in disappointment before stepping forward again. "Deaf, too. That's a shame." Filling the pipet to its limit, Gideon held it over the left nipple, his eyes unwavering from hers as he let it drip over the puckered flesh.

"*Fuck*. Fuck, fuck." She tried to twist away again. "Why the fuck do you care?"

"Don't you think somebody ought to?"

She reeled back as though he'd slapped her face. "Fuck you."

His foot shot out, catching the spreader bar he'd placed between her ankles and dragging her close to him again. "I guess if Toby was just a pet, you might not care so much," Gideon commented.

Her gaze darted to the glass tube in the bottle as it slowly filled with more holy water and followed it as Gideon reached between her legs. Everything in her froze as he inserted the slim cylinder into her pussy, and for the first time since getting her in chains, Gideon caught a whiff of her fear.

"Who killed Toby Richards?" he asked again, the pipet poised in anticipation of her response.

Tricia didn't answer immediately, and he let a small trickle of water escape the thin tube. Tears filled her eyes, but they never lost the glint of anger. "I did," she whispered.

Though a flash of satisfaction surged through him, Gideon neither reacted nor moved his hand away. "Why?"

She shook her head. "I don't know." Before he released another trickle of water, she added quickly. "Please, I don't know. I don't…I don't remember."

"Guess what?" Gideon said softly. "Pleading amnesia didn't work for Rudolf Hess, either."

When he released another measure of holy water, her screams of pain echoed against the playroom walls.

"I don't remember," she sobbed. "I don't remember any of it. I would never have hurt Toby. Ever."

The tears streaming down her face were a nice touch, Gideon thought. But he held still as he asked, "And why should I believe that? He was just your pet, right? You even took him to Sangre to pass around."

She shook her head from side to side, reminding him of a horse. "You would know something about that, wouldn't you?"

Tricia wasn't going to get to him that easily. "Do you at least remember how you left him?" he asked, ignoring her gibe. "The coroner counted over two dozen fresh puncture wounds, including the ones in his balls. You popped those like a ripe peach apparently. Tell me. Did they taste good?"

"I don't remember." She was sobbing again. "I don't remember. I don't even remember taking it that night. I wasn't touching the stuff."

The soft intake of Jesse's breath behind him made Gideon pause. She had to be talking about obsidian. It was an even more graphic reminder of how dangerous the drug could be.

"I find that hard to believe," Gideon said. "Henry's supplying obsidian to half the vamps in town. Are you trying to tell me you never tried it?"

"Not when I was with Toby. Never with him." She took a huge, unneeded breath that turned into another sob. "And Henry wouldn't let me when I was packing for him. Do you know what he'll do to me if he found out I was hyped up? I wasn't even supposed to have any that night…"

"Interesting story. I'd almost believe it if I didn't know that obsidian doesn't make you forget."

"I lost myself," she said, her voice cracking. Her hair was covering her face, but when she looked up again, her eyes were dead. "Do you think if I knew what I was doing, I could have hurt him? Do you think… Do you think…" She ducked her head. "Do what you want. It doesn't matter."

Her grief was palpable, but Gideon knew that if he conceded to it now, he wouldn't get anything more from her. Though he didn't remove the holy water from inside her, he kept his voice low. "What made Toby Richards so special?"

"Everything…everything…we were in love."

"But you killed him anyway. Because you were high on obsidian." He paused, trying to block out the sudden influx of memories, the smell of Jesse as Gideon pinned him to the building in that dark alley, the thud of his heartbeat against his tongue as he'd swallowed draught after draught of his blood. He'd told Jess he didn't want to kill him, but now, he saw how lucky they were that he hadn't been even more exposed than he had. "If you didn't take it, then how did you get high?"

"I…everything is…I went to the warehouse to see Henry. He said that he didn't need me. I was free to go. So I went to see Toby. That's all that happened. And then the next day…the next morning…I…woke up…and…"

He was glad she wasn't looking at him. It was getting harder to retain a neutral façade. "And…?"

"And…I saw him. It was too late, so I ran. If Henry…he would know and he'd think I was stealing from him…"

Gideon knew all too well how Henry dealt with those he thought betrayed him. Not everybody could be as ballsy as Rina.

He let the pipet slide out an inch, though a good portion still remained inside her channel. "So you've been hiding from Henry? Is that what you're telling me?"

She nodded. "He wouldn't just kill me."

Gideon had the answers he needed for Lucas now. Richards wouldn't be happy that his son's murderer was a vampire and outside his jurisdiction, but at least it would give him peace of mind.

It was time to get the answers Gideon needed.

"Why is Henry doing this?" he asked. "Obsidian is unpredictable and expensive for him to manufacture. What's he hoping to get out of this?"

Tricia laughed bitterly. "You think he tells me anything? He tells me where to go and what to do, and that's it."

He believed her. Henry hadn't attained as much power as he had by being fast and loose with his facts. It had been worth a try, though.

"Then tell me when he uses the warehouse," he said. "I know he's not there all the time."

"Every Wednesday night, every second Sunday night. I don't know what he does there the whole time. That's just when I picked the shit up."

It was good enough for Gideon. He pulled out the pipet and released his hold on the spreader, letting her swing back as her muscles sagged.

"Did you get that, Jess?" he said, without looking away from Tricia.

"Yes," Jesse said, his voice clear but weak. "Every detail."

Regardless of Jesse's earlier assertions, Gideon didn't want him to see anything more, even if there was more to be done. "Then let's get out of here." He tossed the holy water aside and headed for the door. "Tricia needs to do some thinking about what she's done."

Jesse followed him silently, not stopping even when Gideon paused to shut the door. He made it halfway down the stairs before coming to an abrupt halt and turning around. "You're not leaving her hanging in there."

Gideon frowned. "I'm not going to let her go, Jess. I can still use her."

"You don't have to let her go, but you can't leave her hanging there like that. I know you can keep her without treating her that way."

"I thought we agreed you weren't going to intervene."

Jesse folded his arms. "I'm not intervening. I didn't intervene. But what possible good could come from leaving her hanging like that? My

God, Gideon, what difference does it make to you if she's not hanging from the fucking ceiling? I know you have a cage that can hold her."

"Because if I coddle her now, she's going to know she's got the upper hand. What if we need more information? I need her to know this is my show, not hers."

"What if she's told you everything she knows? I may not know a great deal about keeping an upper hand and scaring the fuck out of people, but I do know a girl who's beaten when I see her. She doesn't care. The person she loves is dead, and she thinks she's as good as dead. Either you'll kill her or Henry will." Jesse marched over to his desk. "And what was her great sin, Gideon?"

Anger rippled through his every word. It was the reaction Gideon had feared.

"She killed a man, remember? She did more than kill him. You read the coroner's report. He was still alive when she tore into his gut."

Jesse yanked at his collar, revealing the bites on his neck. Even the one that was over a week old still looked deep and red. "I never stopped you because I trusted that you wouldn't leave me an empty husk. Even later that night, when you practically turned me into your chew toy. I would bet money that Toby trusted her the same way, and I believe she never meant to get high on obsidian when she was with him. Henry infected her, Gideon. I don't know why, but I think she's telling the truth. She didn't intend to hurt him."

Gideon wanted to point out that there was a distinct difference between Tricia and himself, but realized as the words poised on his tongue that maybe the difference wasn't as great as he thought. Tricia had tried to hold back because Toby was important to her. It was the exact same reason he'd given himself for protecting Jess.

"One more hour," he said. "Then I'll put her in the cage and give her something to eat. Is that all right?"

Jesse nodded, and it was like Gideon had pulled a plug on his anger. "Yes, thank you. I need...I need to get to work. I'm going to try to make an antidote."

Gideon had already turned away, ready to go back and sit guard on Tricia, when Jesse's final words made him stop. "You can do that?" The possibility had never occurred to him. "Can we do that without hitting John up again?"

"Yeah. Magic is a lot like...food. You can deconstruct it, break it down into the proper components, and make your own recipe. It's not a perfect solution, but I have the resources, and I've done this sort of thing before. But I'm going to be handling the obsidian, which means I either need to go home, or you need to avoid going downstairs while I'm working."

Enough of this entire operation had been taken out of Jesse's hands. Gideon knew what he had to do.

"I'll do whatever you tell me to," he said. "If you'll be comfortable taking it home, that's okay. But I'll stay out of your way as long as you need me to if you'd rather work here."

He gestured at his desk. "All my stuff is here. Your bathroom is large enough. I can make a temporary laboratory in there. Hopefully, that'll keep any of the substance from getting airborne."

He hadn't thought about that possibility, and dread settled in his veins like a cold poison. "That's not good enough." At Jesse's frown, he reached into his pocket, pulled out his key ring, and tossed it to Jess. "I'm going to take Tricia down now. I want you to lock both of us in the cage. Just to be safe."

Jesse caught the keys, but he didn't look happy about it. "You want me to lock you up? Gideon, I...are you sure that's a good idea?"

"We're not entirely sure how obsidian even works, Jess. And you heard Tricia. She didn't realize what was going on until it was too late. I am *not* going to let you turn out like Toby Richards." On an instinct, he crossed the distance between them and rested a hand on Jesse's shoulder. It felt important to gain that physical contact, though such a simple touch wasn't what Gideon really wanted. "Do this for me. For both of us."

Jesse looked down at his hand where it rested on his shoulder. He reached up, wrapping his fingers around Gideon's and giving them a soft squeeze. "Okay. If I don't have it figured out by this time tomorrow, I'm going to take it all home and finish there."

"Sounds like a plan."

Gideon hoped it actually worked.

CHAPTER 13

It was just as well that Gideon was secure in a cage, because Jesse didn't want to talk to him. He kept thinking about the girl—the vampire—sobbing about the boy she loved, hanging miserably in the interrogation room. Fortunately, he had a good excuse to bury himself in work and obsess over something other than the vampire. Which meant, of course, that Jess couldn't stop thinking about him

He slept for a few hours, but his dreams were covered in thick black fluid, like tar, and when he woke up, he felt sick to his stomach. He needed to find an antidote, needed to figure out a way to deliver the substance, and why hadn't he paid attention to all the lectures from his father about the shared properties of magic and chemistry? He didn't eat. He couldn't. His appetite had disappeared when he smelled Tricia's nipples burning under the holy water.

It had been over a day, and she was still upstairs. Still imprisoned with Gideon, still burned, probably still crying. He occasionally drifted upstairs to check on them, and Gideon might have been angry. Not smoldering angry. Not threateningly so. But angry enough that the air sparked every time Jess neared the cage. Or maybe that was Jesse's own rage, reacting against Gideon, causing the hair on the back of his hands to stand on end.

Despite his heated emotions, he wasn't spoiling for a fight. Even when he sealed the obsidian away and decided it was safe to free Gideon, he couldn't even really talk to him. He couldn't bring himself to speak to Gideon because he didn't know how to explain his reaction.

The questions racing in his mind weren't: *How could Gideon do such a thing? How could Gideon hurt her like that?* The questions he couldn't let go of were: H*ow can I still love him so much? What kind of person am I?*

And he was afraid. He trusted Gideon so completely that it was impossible to imagine a world where doubt was allowed to exist. He'd never thought twice about the times Gideon had bitten him, but how much danger was he really in? Would Gideon wake up one morning, shocked to find Jesse's mauled and desecrated corpse in the bed with him? And why wasn't that thought enough to send him packing? Why had he surrendered so much of himself to Gideon that he couldn't even walk away for a few days?

"I made coffee."

Gideon's voice cut through his preoccupation, and Jess looked up to see him standing at the bottom of the stairs. He had showered and changed, his hair damp where it fell against his brow. The scratches Tricia had left on his face were gone already. In fact, there was no visible evidence of her capture and interrogation at all, and it only made Jesse's stomach churn even more.

"Thanks," he said, though he didn't ask for any, and he didn't stand up to pour his own. Gideon didn't walk away, like he expected Jesse to add something else. "I should have something to show for my efforts by tomorrow."

"Have you slept at all?"

"I got a few hours last night. I'll take a nap later."

"If you're not up to driving, you can always crash in my bed."

Jesse leaned back in his chair. "No, Gideon, I don't think I can."

A shadow passed over Gideon's face, and he advanced a step closer. "If this is about what happened last night…"

Jesse sighed, weighing the pros and cons of broaching the subject. On the one hand, Gideon would probably hound him until he agreed to talk. On the other, the sun was still up, and he could escape to safety and delay the inevitable. But if he did that, there would be a negative impact on the work they actually needed to do.

"It is. But it's not about you."

Everything in him tightened when Gideon closed the rest of the distance to perch on the corner of his desk. "Then what is it?"

"That your skin still reeked of her burnt flesh yesterday, yet I still would have kissed you without a second thought."

Gideon's head bowed, and Jess was grateful for the momentary reprieve from his steady regard. "I did what I had to do, Jess. You know that."

"And I don't blame you for that. I don't. But I can't stop thinking about it. It feels like there was a line that I didn't even know about until I crossed it." And what would Michelle think if she knew of this conversation? Would she claim this wasn't going to be the first line he would cross?

That brought Gideon's attention back to him. "What makes you think you did? You didn't touch Tricia. You even stepped up to help her."

"She was frightened and she lost somebody important to her. I can't even imagine what it must feel like to take the life of somebody you love. Something horrible was done to her. There ought to have been another way. And I took it for granted that there wasn't."

"Jess..." Gideon stopped. His brows drew into a dark line as his mind worked. "When everything is said and done, Tricia's still a vampire. A vampire who deals drugs, who kills without thought of consequence. Yeah, it would've been nice to get what we needed without resorting to...what I did, but let's face it. Nothing else would've worked. Look at what it took to get her to even admit she'd killed Toby." He leaned forward, his gaze suddenly impassioned. "There *was* no other way. And it is *not* a reflection on you that I did what I had to. So stop thinking that."

Jesse knew Gideon was right. He also knew he couldn't explain the real crux of the issue. It would be easier if he could just blurt that he loved Gideon, and for the first time since making that realization, he was actually coming to terms with what it meant. The world was violent and messy, and love made things worse, not better.

He nodded. "I know. And you're right about Tricia. She's not some innocent girl off the street. Maybe I'm just tired." *And scared.* Glancing up, he noticed there were still drops of water running from Gideon's hair, down his neck. "Maybe I do need to crash in your bed for a while, after all."

He was gently pulled to his feet when Gideon suddenly took his hand and tugged. There was a moment of vertigo, but it was just as much from the contact of Gideon's fingers as it was to the rush of blood inside him. It was made worse when Gideon stood as well and pulled his body flush with his in a tight hug. Then all his blood reversed direction and ran straight to his cock.

"You're a good man," Gideon whispered in his ear. "And it's a privilege to be able to call you my best friend."

Jesse warmed, the pleasure at Gideon's words more powerful than any doubts he might have had. He didn't need Gideon's assurances that he was a good person, but the reminder that Gideon genuinely cared for him—even if it wasn't the way he cared for Gideon—was enough to convince him he was doing the right thing by staying.

Sighing softly, he turned his head and skimmed his mouth over Gideon's neck, collecting the drops of water he had noticed earlier.

Gideon's chest rumbled against his body, a sound of satisfaction if Jess had ever heard one. His large hands splayed across his back and ass, and when Gideon tilted his head a fraction to encourage more contact with his neck, Jesse was more than happy to comply. Every soft caress against the sinew made the cock pressing to his harden even more, and he allowed himself the luxury of exploring the sculpture of Gideon's back through his thin shirt.

"Did you want company when you crash?" he heard Gideon murmur.

"I think I would like some company, yes," Jesse said, pausing only long enough to answer before resuming his exploration of Gideon's neck. It felt like he couldn't get enough of the way Gideon tasted, the way his skin felt. He wanted to sample much more than Gideon's neck.

Gideon bowed his head, and Jess shuddered at the first touch of his mouth against the healing bite marks. "There was only one thing I didn't like about watching you swallow all those cocks at Sangre." The tip of his tongue traced the small punctures. "None of them were mine."

"You know all you have to do is say the word," Jess said, his hands going to Gideon's fly. "Any time."

Gideon grabbed his wrist, stopping him from undoing the zipper. "Not here." He gave one last lick of the marks before pulling back. "It's probably time I made good on my promise to tie you to my bed, don't you think?"

A chill raced down Jesse's spine. How many times had he thought about that very thing? Of course, if he was tied to the bed, he wouldn't get the chance to taste every square inch of Gideon's body, but the trade-off was fair. "It *is* about time to make good on that promise."

Gideon's mouth curved into a sly smile as he led Jess back to the stairs. He didn't say a word, but that was probably a good thing. Every step closer to Gideon's bedroom made Jesse's pulse pound louder in his ears, blocking out everything else but the thrilling anticipation of what was to come.

Gideon only released Jesse's wrist when the door was closed behind them. "Strip," he said, going around the far side of the bed. Jess watched as he pulled out the strap from beneath the mattress corner, and his cock throbbed even more. "Then lie down. You haven't had enough time to recoup for serious fun, but that doesn't mean there aren't other games we can play."

Jesse grimaced at the reminder of his fragile, mortal body. He wished his flesh could keep up with his desires—with Gideon's desires. He had stepped tantalizingly close to the edge a few times, like a man who wasn't quite suicidal, but sought the thrill of a long fall.

He liked the way Gideon watched him as he undressed. Jess wasn't a particularly shy person, but he always felt a little timid under Gideon's intense, hungry gaze. He didn't speak until he was naked on the bed. "What sort of games do you have in mind?"

"Games of anticipation instead of pain."

His grasp was strong as he stretched Jesse's arm to the corner of the bed, binding it in the thick Velcro strap. Quickly, he did the same to the other wrist and both ankles, and then went to his dresser. Jesse's view was blocked as Gideon slid open the top drawer, but soon enough, he saw the leather flogger Gideon removed, and a fired sizzle went straight to his cock.

"I'm not going to hurt you," Gideon said, standing at the side of the bed. His gaze settled on the hard column of Jesse's length. Loosely, he held the flogger over it and began making circular motions with his wrist, dragging the very tips of the leather strips feathered around Jess' cock. "I'm going to make you want it so badly that you're screaming."

Jesse looked pointedly at his cock, already dully glistening with pre-come. "How hard do you think that's going to be?"

"Doesn't matter." His hungry grin accompanied the soft brush of the flogger along Jesse's smooth balls. "The best part is hearing you scream anyway."

He knew Gideon would keep him tied to the bed until he screamed himself hoarse, and he had very little problem with that. Jesse squirmed as Gideon continued to caress him with the very tips of the leather strands, wiggling against the smooth, silk sheets. Everything was a soft caress. Barely touching, barely teasing, and yet, it felt sharp, a direct assault on his senses. He realized that before he screamed for Gideon to touch him, he'd be begging to feel the sting of the flogger against his sensitive skin.

"I love the way your cock and balls look shaved," Gideon murmured. "I can already feel what they're going to taste like on my tongue."

Jesse moaned softly, Gideon's words setting off a chain reaction of images in his mind. If Gideon kept talking like that, he wouldn't need to use the flogger. Jesse would scream, beg, whimper, and make any number of promises to feel Gideon's tongue anywhere on him.

Gideon shifted, dragging the flogger up his twitching abdomen. "This is one of my favorite toys. It's why I keep it up here. There's nothing like lashing someone and then sucking their hot skin into my mouth. It makes all the blood rush to the surface and then when I finally get into you, it feels like you explode."

"Oh?" Jesse asked, his best attempt at a response. It felt like he should have some sort of answer to that, even if his balls were throbbing. Gideon had just mentioned several of his favorite things— the sting of the flogger, Gideon's mouth, and Gideon finally getting into him. "But you're not going to do that today?"

Slowly, Gideon shook his head. The leather strips were now trailing along Jesse's chest, flicking over his nipples. "But it'll happen. I promise. I want the luxury of pounding into you for hours when it does."

Jesse's nipples hardened into peaks, and he tilted his head back as the flogger moved higher. His entire body shook as Gideon teased one of the bite marks, confusing his nerve endings with the teasing pressure on a spot marked for pain. "When do you think that'll be?"

"When you least expect it."

The sharp crack of the flogger made Jess jump, but the leather hit the sheet next to his ear, close enough for him to feel the whistle of air. Above him, Gideon's dark eyes gleamed, and the tip of his tongue appeared as it ran along his teeth.

"I dreamed about drinking you last night," he said. "I almost asked you to let me out this morning when you brought me my blood."

Jesse swallowed hard, noticing the way Gideon watched his throat working. "What happened in your dream?"

"You were in the cage instead of me." Tossing aside the flogger, Gideon took a step away from the bed and dropped his hand to his belt. "Tricia had escaped, and I'd locked you in there to keep you safe while I looked for her. When I came back, you'd stripped out of your clothes and were pressing up to the bars, your cock sticking out between the bars while you slowly jerked off."

And just like that, Jesse decided that he would need to spend some time in that cage. In fact, as his cock twitched, he wondered if it wasn't one of Gideon's finer ideas. "Did you let me out of the cage?"

Gideon undid his pants and pushed them down, the hem of his shirt draping over his jutting shaft when he straightened again. "No. I got down on my knees and grabbed your ass to pull you even tighter against the bars. And then I sucked on your balls while you continued to work on your cock."

Jesse caught his breath and curled his fingers into his palm. He liked being at Gideon's mercy—loved it—but it killed him that he couldn't touch Gideon, especially when he was standing so close and he still smelled of fresh soap. "I…really like this dream."

"You should've seen it." Jesse was riveted by Gideon's fingers as they undid the buttons on his shirt, slowly exposing the hard wall of his upper body. "You came all over my face. And then I licked a path up your stomach until I got to your nipple." Gideon tossed the shirt away. "That's where I bit you."

Jesse opened his mouth to speak, but all that escaped was a high, reedy sound from the back of his throat. The corner of Gideon's mouth lifted, and Jesse swallowed to try again. "Gideon, if you'd like, I can start screaming for you now."

"Really?" Gideon feigned confusion as he climbed onto the bed to straddle one of Jesse's thighs. "But I haven't even done anything yet. Or at least…" Grasping his cock at the base, he touched the wet tip to Jesse's before dragging it down his length and to his balls. "…not very much."

"No, no, trust me." Jesse arched off the bed, straining for more contact. "You've done enough."

Gideon chuckled. "That's for me to decide. And I decide…I'm not done yet."

He let go of his cock and skimmed his fingers along Jesse's inner thigh, crawling at an inexorable pace upward. Goosebumps erupted along Jesse's skin as it alternated hot and cold at the soft caress. Before Gideon reached the sac, however, he switched to the other leg, repeating the motion with the same tempo, the same silken pressure.

Jesse watched with growing horror as Gideon switched to his other thigh once again, roamed over his hips, his lower abdomen, and then circled the base of his cock with his thumb. He couldn't take it any more, his eyes rolling back. Gideon would probably keep this up for hours, finding new, tiny sensitive spots. *Like that one. And that one.*

Jesse jerked and hissed. *And that one.*

"I love the noises you make," Gideon murmured.

The weight from his thigh lifted away, and Jess opened his eyes to see Gideon climbing up his body until his knees were on either side of his waist. He didn't sit, though, keeping all contact away from Jesse's cock. His thumb circled a nipple, but his eyes were no longer assessing the flesh he touched. They were too busy boring into Jesse's.

"Do you dream about me?"

"All the time," Jesse answered without hesitation.

Gideon switched to the other nipple. "What do I do to you in them?"

It would have been easier to say what Gideon didn't do to him. "You suck my cock. You let me suck you. You fuck me until I can't walk. You bite me...everywhere." His dreams were usually blood-soaked, come-soaked affairs that made it hard to get a decent night's sleep. "You've fucked me on every square inch of every available surface in the apartment, the office, the car..."

Gideon edged forward, his balls dragging along Jesse's chest. Reaching out, he brushed his thumb over Jess' lower lip, but the instant Jess opened his mouth to suck it in, Gideon withdrew his hand. He waited, poised, until Jess closed his mouth, and then stretched again to caress his lips. "What's your favorite fantasy?"

Gideon might as well have asked to pick his favorite star in the sky. "Today? I'm wearing nothing but my collar and leash, I'm at your complete beck and call, and the come on my face and in my ass barely has time to dry before you're ready for me again."

He chuckled. "That's definitely fantasy, Jess, because when it does happen, my come isn't going to have time to dry. In case you haven't noticed, my turnaround time is mostly nonexistent. One of the pluses of vampire stamina."

"I stand corrected. What are the other pluses of vampire stamina?"

"Oh, sitting here and tormenting you forever."

Jesse released his breath in a long sigh. "Please don't do that, Gideon. Please. I can't take it."

"You're selling yourself short." Gideon fisted his cock, giving it long, languorous pulls that Jess couldn't tear his eyes away from. "But never say I'm not willing to discuss it. If I don't torment you, what should I do instead?"

Jesse licked his lips. "Feed me your cock." His eyes darted to Gideon's face. "Please, Gideon. I need to taste you. That's all I want to do."

"That's all?" His hand stilled, his free one coming up and catching a drop of pre-come from the tip. With a wicked smirk, he pressed the finger to Jesse's mouth, who promptly parted his lips to suck it inside. "So that should mean you're fine now, right?"

"No." In contrast to Gideon's teasing tone, Jesse sounded dead serious. "I'm not fine now. I won't be fine until you slide your cock down my throat."

He saw the flash of lust darken Gideon's eyes the second before Gideon started moving. "Let's start with you licking my balls," he said, positioning himself over Jesse's head. He held his cock up, the heavy sac lowering to Jess' mouth. "And I'll think about it."

Jesse was eager to take what he could get, parting his lips before Gideon even finished speaking. He lapped at Gideon's skin, drawing the sac into his mouth. He alternately sucked and licked, relishing the taste of Gideon's skin, the way he smelled, the soft moans of encouragement. His own balls were aching for the same sort of attention, but he ignored that pain—it didn't seem to matter when he was this close to getting what he wanted anyway.

Gideon slipped his hand beneath Jesse's neck, supporting him so that he could reach without strain. His broad thumb caressed below Jesse's jaw, following each muscle as it worked, occasionally straying to tease the corner of his mouth. When Jess sucked harder, tightening the suction around both balls until the skin stretched and strained, Gideon stiffened, a groan rumbling through his body. Jess assumed he was stopping to relish the pleasure.

"I love how hot your mouth gets," he murmured. His eyes shone where they met Jesse's. "It's been awhile since I had a human lover, but it hasn't been like this since…" A shudder ran through him, and he lifted up, his sac popping audibly out of Jesse's mouth. "No more playing. Tell me you want it."

"I do," Jess breathed. "Give it to me, Gideon. Please. And I'll show you everything I didn't get a chance to do at Sangre."

Gideon let out a slow hiss. Curling his hand around the root of his cock, he leaned forward and grasped the headboard, tilting his hips to drag the wet tip across Jesse's lips.

The second his tongue touched Gideon's cock, a thrill went down his spine. He hadn't missed what Gideon had almost said. He could dwell on the possible implications of that later, but now he wanted to show Gideon how good he could be. How good *this* could be. He lifted his head as high as possible, taking in Gideon's cock almost to the root, and hollowed his cheeks as he waited for Gideon to lower himself farther.

"Take it slow," Gideon coaxed. He pulled back, letting Jesse's lips drag along his shaft until they reached the crown. When Jess swirled his tongue around the ridge, Gideon groaned and began thrusting forward. "Fuck. You're going to make this hard for me, aren't you?"

I'm going to sure as hell try. Jesse kept Gideon's admonishment to take it slow in mind, relaxing against the pillow so Gideon had complete control of the pace. He closed his mouth slightly as Gideon pulled out, scraping his teeth along his shaft until he reached Gideon's head. He slid his tongue along the bottom, then pushed the tip into Gideon's slit, coaxing out more sticky fluid.

"That's it, just like that, keep going, keep going…" Gideon pushed a little harder, nudging against the back of Jesse's throat. He reached down and brushed the hair off Jess' brow before placing the heel of his hand against it. "Time to go deeper, boy. Now, breathe."

He automatically took a deep breath, the tone of Gideon's voice making his blood roar in his ears. As soon as he did, Gideon pushed his cock down Jesse's throat, not stopping until Jesse's nose was brushing against his skin. Jesse's hands curled tightly, his nails digging into his palms, until pain radiated down his arm. Jesse wanted nothing more than to grip Gideon's thighs and hold him there.

The force of Gideon's hand kept Jess from following his cock when he pulled back, but Gideon didn't hesitate to thrust back in, pushing past his nonexistent defenses to sink into his throat again. Jess swallowed, and Gideon curled his fingers into his scalp, nails scraping against the skin.

After another two or three slow, torturous thrusts that left Jess helpless again, Gideon began to pick up speed. Jesse was completely overwhelmed, and he was almost tempted to close his eyes, but he didn't want to look away from Gideon for a second. He kept Jesse immobile, and Jess responded by increasing the suction around his shaft and humming, sending vibrations through Gideon's cock.

"I fucking love your mouth," Gideon chanted. "Going to make you choke on my come, go so deep, you'll feel it in your balls, boy. And you'll love it, I know you will. You'll beg me to do it again and again and again until your throat is raw and your lips are numb."

The muscles in Gideon's abdomen tensed, and his thrusts became erratic. With every stroke, his sac slapped against Jesse's chin. Then his head dropped back, a guttural shout splitting the air, and he shoved one final time into Jesse's mouth, harder, deeper, his cock pulsing as he started shooting even before he hit Jesse's throat.

The warm liquid didn't take Jesse by surprise, but for a moment, he thought he might choke. Gideon's cock kept jerking, and Jesse's throat worked frantically, swallowing every bit. Even as Gideon began to pull away from him, Jess realized he was right. He would beg for it again and again.

He thought Gideon would stop, but he didn't, he kept pulling back and back, sliding his body down until he stretched atop Jess. As Jess was about to swallow the last of the come clinging to his tongue, Gideon curled his hand around his throat and said, "Don't." In the next moment, his mouth slammed to Jesse's, searching to taste him.

Gideon didn't release him as he deepened the kiss, and Jesse's head started to spin. The taste of his come, the force of Gideon's tongue, the strong fingers against his skin, and Gideon's cock, still hard, sliding against his thigh were all almost enough to make him explode. Gideon kissed him until there wasn't a trace left in his mouth, and then swept his tongue through Jesse's mouth once more, slowly, before lifting his head.

"Sometimes I think I could live in there," he murmured, his fingers stroking the side of Jesse's neck.

Jesse tilted his head back slightly, encouraging Gideon to continue. He thought he would be somewhat satisfied, but desire still gnawed at him. He knew Gideon could feel how hard his cock was, knew he could smell his arousal and hear his pulse hammering.

Using his hold on Jesse's neck, Gideon turned his head to the side, exposing his first bite mark. "I have to say, I hate the idea of obsidian." He bowed down and licked across the puncture wounds, sending a cascade of shivers through Jesse's helpless body. "But it did do one thing." He ground their cocks together. "It got us doing what we should've been doing years ago."

"Yes, yes," Jesse panted, in agreement with every word. He jerked his hips, grinding against Gideon again. "Please, Gideon…can I please come?"

Gideon finally released his throat, sliding his palm down Jesse's side to grip his hip. "Since you ask so nicely…"

Jess missed his weight as he rose above him, but his heart thudded wildly as he realized what Gideon was going to do. With a last leer tossed over his shoulder, Gideon reversed his position, dangling his still-hard cock over Jesse's mouth again as he cupped Jesse's balls.

"So smooth," he heard Gideon murmur. "And all for me."

All the air whooshed out of his chest as he finally felt Gideon's mouth, the soft swipe of his tongue around his sac as he slowly sucked it past his lips.

Jesse stuck his tongue out, licking and lipping Gideon's smooth skin, but it was difficult to concentrate. Gideon's mouth was surprisingly warm, and his tongue was rough, his lips tight, and now Jesse finally gave into the impulse to close his eyes. The taste of Gideon's cock, and the way he seemed to want to taste every inch of Jesse's balls did not help the ache in his groin. The throbbing spread through his body and everything from his toes to his fingertips pulsed, and still Gideon sucked on his sac, apparently in no hurry to shift his attention to Jesse's cock.

A strong hand stroked along Jesse's inner thigh, finding the same path it had taken earlier. His muscles twitched, fighting against the ticklish sensation, but when it reached the sweaty junction separating leg from hip, it didn't stop. It didn't stop until it reached the skin behind his balls, and then it veered downward to trace the hot crack of his ass.

Jesse caught his breath and tensed, trying to focus on Gideon's cock when all he could think about was the path Gideon's finger was taking. As soon as he pressed through the pucker, Jesse clenched, gradually relaxing as Gideon pressed deeper, then added a second finger. That was too much.

"Gideon...please...please...I can't...can't take this...please need you..."

The words were cut off by the sudden lift of Gideon's hips and the even more sudden drive of his cock past Jesse's lips. Gideon didn't stop, pushing down his throat, but even as he began ruthlessly fucking his face, Gideon abandoned Jesse's balls and shifted to swallow his shaft down in a single stroke. There was no pausing, no time to adjust. He hollowed out his cheeks and began humming as his head and fingers moved at the same swift rhythm.

Jesse moaned with every thrust, completely carried away by the hard rhythm Gideon established. The hint of Gideon's come once again at the back of his throat sent him closer to the edge, but it was his fast fingers and the glorious vibrations going through his cock that sent him flying over it. He couldn't shout around Gideon's cock, but the sound filled his chest as he erupted in Gideon's throat.

Within seconds, Gideon's come was filling his mouth, but so caught up in his orgasm, Jesse couldn't catch it all, sticky droplets seeping out the corners of his lips. Gideon ground his balls into Jess' nose, the scent musky and mouth-watering, and though he pulled his fingers from Jesse's sore hole, he kept a tight suction around Jesse's cock until it began to soften. Only then did Gideon disengage, twisting around to once again cover Jesse's body with his own.

"And here I thought you'd never waste a drop of my come," he scolded with a smile. He leaned down and licked the fluid running down Jesse's jaw. "We're going to have to practice that."

"Okay," Jesse said, dazed. At that moment, he would probably agree to anything Gideon said they needed to do. Gideon cleaned his mouth and chin thoroughly, then pressed his lips against Jesse's.

"So," Gideon said, when he finally broke the never-ending kiss, "was it worth the wait?"

"It was worth the wait," Jesse breathed. "You've always been worth the wait."

Gideon hesitated, and for a moment, Jess wondered if he'd said too much, gone too far. It was difficult to read Gideon even when he wasn't in an orgasm fog, but now, it was simply impossible.

"You should get some rest now." He peeled away, stretching to undo the heavy Velcro strapping Jesse down, and the next was said with his eyes averted. "If you want me to stay, I will, but I can't promise that you'll get much sleep if that happens."

A part of Jesse didn't care if Gideon stayed and kept him awake all day and all night. But his eyes were already heavy. "Are we going to the warehouse tonight?"

"Yeah. I talked some with Tricia while I was in the cage. I think I've figured out how we're going to tackle this."

Jesse nodded. "Then I better get some sleep so I'm of use for you."

He turned on his side, his eyes falling shut. He waited for the bed to shift and Gideon to leave, but he stretched out beside him. Jesse closed his eyes, and this time, he didn't dream about tar that coated everything.

CHAPTER 14

It was a simple plan. Gideon liked simple. It was hard to fuck up simple.

Go to the warehouse. Jess would take point on the ground level while Gideon searched the inside for human life signs. Get the humans out, though he doubted he'd find any. Burn the warehouse down.

Obsidian problem solved. Henry couldn't deal if it was destroyed and he was dust. Even Jess liked it, which boosted Gideon's confidence in success a thousand percent.

It didn't mean that they weren't going in prepared, though. Gideon stood out of the way as Jesse finished tucking stakes into his light jacket.

"Stay out of the alley," he said. "I'll block the side entrance before we go in so that it's harder for anybody to try and escape that way. But if you hear something, go to the mouth of it and use the crossbow. You're still sharp, right?"

Jess nodded. "I don't always sit behind that desk, you know."

He didn't like Jess engaging in the fights, but occasionally, circumstances demanded it. Gideon didn't want anybody escaping with obsidian, and if that meant killing every vampire who tried to escape, then so be it. Besides, Jess was a good shot with the crossbow. It was one of the reasons Gideon had hired him in the first place. If there was anybody he trusted with long-range weaponry, it was Jess.

Still, he watched him prepare the crossbow out of the corner of his eye anyway, watched his long, slim fingers deftly manipulate the small bolts, searched for any sign that he might not be as ready as Gideon needed him to be. Jess didn't falter. Not once.

The drive to the warehouse was quiet and tense, both men too focused on the events to come than to consider events already past. Jess had slept most of the day away while Gideon consolidated the plan, but every once in awhile, the temptation to talk to him about what had happened between them—what *was* happening—tickled at the edges of Gideon's thoughts.

The sex was amazing. Surprising. Jesse was amazing and surprising. And each time Gideon touched him, each time Jess looked at him through those thick lashes with eyes gleaming in lust and adoration, Gideon fell for him a little bit harder. It was one thing to love Jess as the best friend he'd had in a very long time, but to have that same man who commandeered his professional respect be one of the most satisfying and thrilling partners he'd had in his bedroom as well…

Maybe it was just the newness of it all. Maybe finally unleashing secret passions for each other just made them hungrier. But Gideon didn't think so. And the more time he spent with Jesse, the more convinced he became that it wasn't just desire and a submissive streak a mile wide that Jess was harboring. More than once, he thought he'd heard something deeper in Jesse's tone, words he wanted to say couched in safer terms. There were the glances when he thought Gideon wasn't paying attention, the way his skin would pink with heat when Gideon returned a smile. Separately, they were nothing, fragments of daily life that could hold any kind of meaning at all. But added together, tossed with Gideon's gut reaction, he thought they meant something much, much more.

He turned onto Palm far too soon. Gideon wasn't done trying to sort out the amalgam of emotions inside his head, but there was the warehouse, and here was Jess asking yet again if Gideon was ready, and it was time to work, not play.

"I'm ready," he replied as he pulled to down the street. They didn't want to get too close and be spotted before it was time. "Let's do this."

They walked in silence down the sidewalk. The storm had done little to erase the oppressive heat, and Gideon smelled the sweat already rising to the surface of Jesse's skin. When they passed beneath a streetlight, he saw the small beads glistening on the man's brow, but he didn't say a word until they were standing at the top of the alley.

"Don't let your trigger finger slip," he warned good-naturedly.

Jess smiled and lifted a hand to his forehead. "These things never happen when it's cool outside," he said, wiping away some of the sweat.

"Given this or six feet of lake effect snow, I'll take the heat." Gideon glanced around, but other than a few cars parked in the distance, the neighborhood was just as dead as it had been every other time he'd visited. "What do you think? You think Tricia's right about Henry being here tonight? Or was she just yanking my chain?"

"She believed what she told us. If he's not here, it's through no fault of hers."

"He better be here," Gideon muttered. He wanted this whole debacle done. "Go. I shouldn't be gone long."

He waited until he saw Jess get into position in the shadows near the front door. Then Gideon crept down the alley, his steps practiced and silent. Stopping at the fire escape that snaked up the side of the building, he leapt upward to grab the rail, swinging over its edge with feral grace. The iron bars rattled slightly under his weight, but Gideon didn't pause and pushed open the window he knew led into a back room.

Dust swirled around his feet as he strode through the cramped space. With the building next door blocking any ambient light from the street, the room was near pitch, forcing Gideon to vamp out and heighten his senses. As soon as he did, the stench of obsidian assaulted his nose, and a growl rose unbidden in the back of his throat.

At least he knew Henry was here. From the smell of it, they were cooking up more of the drug. Before reaching for the doorknob, Gideon pulled his gloves out of his pockets and slipped them on. He wasn't going to fall for that trick twice.

He prowled through the corridor, listening for any signs of activity. Revenants echoed back at him, empty rooms following empty rooms, and beyond the obsidian lingering in the air, there was no other evidence of life. He came to the stairs that led down to the ground floor and larger, open warehouse space, but didn't hesitate to start descending. It made better sense for them to be down there anyway. There were easier means of escape on the first level and greater room to work.

Gideon heard it before he'd reached the bottom step.

A breath. Followed by another.

He froze. Listened. Golden eyes searched the darkness.

The breaths were not singular events. It was the constant pulse of someone's inhalations, and not a demon someone.

His nostrils flared.

Human.

Fuck.

Gideon stepped silently off the stairs and turned in the sound's direction. In the distance, he could now make out the rough chatter of a group of people, casual tones and the occasional laugh enough to let him know it had to be Henry and his gang. The human was heading in the same direction, but the even pacing of his heart didn't betray fear or anxiety. There wasn't even a hint of hurrying.

He recognized the scent the moment before his hand clamped over the man's mouth and yanked him back against Gideon's chest.

"What the fuck are you doing here, Lucas?" Gideon growled into the man's ear.

Lucas Richards struggled in the hold, but even in his prime, he was nowhere near a match for Gideon's superior strength. He sagged within seconds, allowing Gideon to drag him backward, away from the congregation of vampires deeper inside the warehouse, until Gideon felt the front door at his ass. Reaching behind, he knocked on it twice, the signal to Jess that it was him and not someone to be staked, before twisting the knob and pulling Lucas out into the street.

Though he didn't worry Jess would shoot, Gideon made sure he blocked Lucas' body from potential harm until Jess lowered his weapons. Only then did Gideon shove Lucas away, glowering as the man stumbled against the wall.

"Not exactly your neighborhood, now is it?" he said. "Are you trying to get yourself killed?"

Lucas straightened, pulling at his polo as he tried to neaten his appearance. "I thought *somebody* should be investigating this place," he spat. "Since it's very clear to me that hiring you was a mistake."

"And you think I like crawling around in a smelly warehouse in the middle of the night just because I'm a vampire?" Gideon snorted, shaking his head. "Go home, Lucas. This is not someplace you want to be tonight."

Jesse stepped between the two angry men, sending a sympathetic glance to Gideon before turning to Lucas. "Councilman Richards, this is a very dangerous place. You could get injured, or worse, if you stay."

"Like Toby, you mean?" For a moment, Lucas actually looked his age, the lines around his eyes deeper, his cheeks hollowed. "I just want answers, damn it. Why won't you tell me what's going on?"

"I know you do. We don't have the answers you want right now. I can tell you the monsters who are responsible for your son's death are in there, and if Gideon hadn't found you, you'd be in ribbons right now. Gideon's right, you should go home."

But Lucas didn't hear the warning. His attention had shifted as soon as Jesse admitted that Toby's killers—indirect killers, but responsible, just the same—still lurked inside the building. Gideon grabbed his arm the moment he saw Lucas tense and pulled him further away from the door.

"You want answers?" he said, his voice low. "Here's one. If you stick around, the headline in tomorrow's paper is going to be 'Councilman found in warehouse fire, foul play suspected.'"

Lucas paled, but didn't flinch. "I want them brought to justice, Gideon."

"They're vampires. This is as close to justice as you're going to get."

"Gideon…"

Jesse's warning came a second too late. They were both too distracted by Lucas to hear the vampires approach. They flung the door open, narrowly missing Jesse with the heavy steel. Jess scrambled back, trying to bring his crossbow level for a shot, and Gideon pushed Lucas aside, putting himself between the unarmed man and the stream of Henry's goons coming out of the warehouse.

The nearest vampire, a guy with a large silver stud through his nose, burst into dust less than a yard away from where Gideon and Lucas stood. Jesse stood behind him, his face set in a grim frown, his body already turning to take aim at the next one.

Lucas shrank against the wall, making himself even smaller. Out of the corner of his eye, Gideon saw him start inching away, but there was no time to stop him before two smaller vamps tried to play wishbone with Gideon's arms. With a snarl, Gideon threw one off, sending him into the street. Jess had a bolt through his heart the second he hit the cement. The second was a bit more tenacious, fangs tearing through Gideon's thin shirt to slice at his skin.

Gideon glanced up to see Jesse trying to take aim at the vampire attacking him, but he wasn't firing. It didn't take long to realize it was because he was worried about hitting the wrong vampire. Narrowing his eyes, Jesse's finger moved over the trigger, as Gideon turned to better position the snarling vamp.

Before Jess could shoot, the crossbow went flying, and Jesse's surprised shout of pain echoed in the narrow alley.

All thoughts of protecting Lucas fled.

Jess is hurt.

Fury, white-hot and livid, surged through Gideon's veins, and he grabbed the throat of the vampire clinging to him and squeezed. His nails broke through the skin, blood seeping out around his fingers, and after a few seconds—though it felt like an eternity—the vamp let go. It was all Gideon needed. The stake was in his hand, through its chest, clattering to the ground as he leapt through the scattering dust toward Jess.

Jesse was pinned against the wall in a defensive position, fending off attacks, but Gideon didn't smell the familiar tang of his blood in the air. He grabbed the back of the vampire's neck and yanked him away from Jesse, then slammed his head against the brick wall. The vamp folded to the ground, blood flowing freely from his shattered skull. Gideon prepared to give him another blow, but Jess freed a stake from his sleeve and shoved it through the vampire's chest. As it burst into dust, Gideon realized they were alone in the alley once again.

"Fuck," he muttered. He scanned the street, just in case he'd been mistaken, but it was still empty. Henry had gotten away. Even Lucas had found time to flee. "*Fuck.*"

"Gideon, are you okay? Are you feeling the effects of the obsidian?"

"What?" Turning back to Jess, Gideon blinked at him twice as the question sank in. "No. No. I don't think so. I'm just pissed we lost him again." His gaze immediately settled on the awkward way Jess was cradling his hand against his body. "God, what about you? What did he do?"

Jess waved him off when he tried to approach. "I'm fine. But we should get out of here. Henry might come back with reinforcements and I won't be able to back you up if there's another fight." He flushed. "I'm sorry."

"Fuck, Jess, stop apologizing."

When Jess started walking back to the car, Gideon scooped up the broken crossbow and trailed after him.

Jess got hurt.

It wasn't until he turned the key in the ignition that he realized he was shaking. He had to grip the steering wheel with white knuckle force in order for Jess not to realize just how badly he'd been affected by what had transpired.

He could've lost Jess.

Getting back to his place was the longest drive Gideon had ever taken.

CHAPTER 15

There had once been a time when Jesse spent at least five or six hours of every twenty-four at his own place. He went back to his apartment to shower, sleep, eat, and change, like a normal person, even when they were in the middle of a case. Now every hour he spent at his own place felt like some sort of bizarre punishment. Gideon hadn't sent him away, of course, but it felt like it.

It took just over thirty-six long hours to perfect his own elixir. Or get it to what he thought was perfection. He still needed to test it—and he didn't think Gideon would be a willing subject, but there was no way he wanted to get caught in a bad situation with an unknown quantity.

It was thick, but not as thick as the elixir used in the obsidian, and it fit in a small spray bottle. He could release the antidote as a mist. Jesse figured that would be the quickest, easiest way to administer a dose. He made enough for two bottles, securing them in his jacket pocket for easy access. It was far too hot for the jacket, but it was a small sacrifice for safety.

As soon as he was finished, he was out the door. It took exactly sixteen minutes to walk to the office from his apartment, and he never varied from his path. The streets were sweating, pulsing with light, but he was alone in the early morning. Of course, he wasn't alone. The vampires and demons were simply lurking beyond his senses.

I should have waited a few hours until dawn.

By the time the thought occurred to him, he was only five minutes away from the office. From Gideon. He put his head down and quickened his pace, his hands buried in his pockets, his fingers brushing against the bottles.

"Hey."

Jesse glanced up, but he didn't stop. "Rina?"

The vampire stepped out of a darkened doorway. "Where's Gideon?"

"Have you been trying to reach him?"

"He's not usually far from you, is he?"

Jesse shrugged. "Do you need something?"

Rina grinned. "Yeah, I do. Do you know what I heard last night?" She began rolling toward him, her hips swaying aggressively.

Jesse held his ground. If she started pushing him, she wouldn't stop until he was cornered.

"No. I didn't."

"I heard that Gideon let everybody play with you but me." Rina pouted. "Does that sound fair to you? After everything I've done? I've been good to Gideon, and he doesn't even invite me to the party."

"There was no party, Rina. But why don't you take that up with Gideon? I'm sure he'd love to talk to you about it."

She was close enough now that he saw her eyes flash yellow, though she still had her blunt teeth. "I don't think we need to get Gideon involved in this, Jess." She said his name like a hiss, dragging it out.

Jesse glanced down the road. He could almost see the office. Five, maybe six more blocks. He didn't think he could win a foot race against a vampire, but if he could get closer to the office maybe he could…What? Scream until Gideon came to rescue him? Why hadn't he thought to bring at least a stake? He had been so absorbed in getting back to Gideon that he hadn't bothered with precautions.

"I think we do." If she took another step, she'd be able to grab him. If she grabbed him, she would overpower him. He took an experimental step back, and she didn't immediately close the space between them. "You do know what Gideon's going to do to you, right?"

She vamped, her fangs startlingly white in the dark night. "I don't care."

That wasn't right. Rina cared. Rina cared a lot about survival. Rina especially cared about not getting on Gideon's bad side. "Are you high?"

"I'm not high." She sprung at him without warning, grabbing his

132

shoulders and dragging him to the ground. She swiped her tongue along his jaw. "I'm flying."

Jesse jerked his head away, but she only chuckled darkly. Pinning him to the ground, she began to writhe, grinding against him. He tried to push her away, but she was too strong as he expected she would be.

Rina looked up, pouting. "Why aren't you hard for me? Monique told me you're one of the best trained pets she ever saw."

Jesse caught his breath. "Oh?"

"Don't worry, though. I know how to get a man hard every time." She ran her tongue over her teeth before ducking her head. "It never fails."

Jesse waited until he almost felt the point of her fang against his skin before jerking his head, smashing his forehead against her temple. She reeled back, howling, no doubt in surprise more than pain. Now that he could move his arms freely, he grabbed her shoulders and butted his head against hers a second time. Blood flowed from her eye and her nose.

He moved quickly while she tried to blink the stars from her eyes, yanking one of the bottles from his pocket and pointing it at her face. He squeezed the trigger with a silent prayer. *Please let this work.*

"Fuck!" She clutched her eyes and began jerking violently. Her elbow connected with his chin, smacking the back of his head against the hard cement.

Jesse barely felt the pain, though as she began to scream, he wondered if his hearing loss would be permanent. He pushed her away and scrambled to his feet, trying to run before he was even fully upright. His ankle throbbed, but it supported his weight. Jess knew he should flee but...did the antidote do anything other than burn?

"Rina?" he tried.

"Get away from me," she shouted.

Enraged, injured vampires were just as deadly as high vampires. And she probably wouldn't want to be interviewed about her current state. Still, he approached. "Are you okay?"

"No, I'm not okay, you fuck! You burned my eyes out."

Jesse frowned. "Let me see."

Rina looked up, but it wasn't to show off her burnt face. She bared her fangs and growled, but the effect was decidedly weaker than she intended. Her eyes weren't burned out, but she was still bleeding, and she suddenly looked very young and deflated.

"Are you going to tell Gideon?" she asked in a small voice.

"I am."

"He's going to kill me."

"You don't care, remember? But if you get up now, you can have a running start."

Rina took off without hesitation, disappearing like another shadow. Jesse didn't watch to see how far she would run. He hurried up the street, moving as fast his throbbing ankle would allow. He kept looking over his shoulder, expecting a vampire, not necessarily Rina, to jump out at him with every step. He didn't stop running until he burst into the office, nearly tripping over his own feet to get into the door.

Gideon stood behind Jesse's desk, leaning over the chair as he used the computer for some unseen purpose. When Jess stumbled inside, Gideon's hand froze on the mouse, but the moment he saw Jesse's dishevelment, he was around the desk, scooping his arm behind Jesse's back as he led him to the nearest chair.

"What the hell happened?" he demanded.

Jesse sank to the chair with a relieved sigh. He felt ten times the better the moment Gideon touched him.

"Rina...I ran into her about six blocks away. She was high on obsidian." Jesse rotated his ankle, but the pain hadn't dulled. "Apparently, Monique told her she was missing out. Anyway, the antidote works."

Gideon knelt on the floor in front of him, picking up his foot and slipping off his shoe. "I'm going to have to have a talk with Monique," he muttered. Though his words were angry, his touch was tender, one strong hand holding the back of Jesse's calf as the other gently worked the joint. "This needs to be iced."

"Yeah." Jesse wasn't terribly concerned about that. Now that he had a chance to process it, the implications of the attack were weighing on him. "I think Monique and whatever she's saying is the least of our problems."

Gideon paused and looked up. His barely controlled anger gleamed in his dark eyes. "You might not think it's a big problem, but I don't want just anybody thinking they can have a piece of you if the whim takes them. They need to know you're off-limits unless I say so."

Jesse nodded, though he still thought Gideon was missing the big picture. He didn't want the vampires of Chicago to think he was free game—but he was surprised that these consequences hadn't occurred to Gideon earlier. "You're right, of course. I'm in full agreement with that. But, Gideon, this stuff is spreading. Rina's one of the last vampires I expected to see using it. And I'm lucky she was alone. It's not going to be safe for anybody to walk the streets anymore."

Understanding dawned in Gideon's face. Setting Jesse's foot down, he straightened and began pacing the length of the room, his brows drawn together into a frown. "Henry's stepping up his game," he said. "This isn't just about having fun in the clubs any more. He wants it everywhere."

Jesse pulled the two spray bottles from his pockets and set them on the table carefully. "Right. Which means whatever we're going to do, we've got to do it soon."

Gideon stopped, his gaze on the antidote. "Is that it?"

"This is it," Jesse said, with more than a hint of pride. "It's in a spray bottle for fast, convenient delivery. The bottle is a little bulky, but I figure I can use something smaller for it, if need be."

"And you're sure it works."

"One second she was trying to kill me, the next I was talking to her and she was just...herself. She claimed it burned, but that might have been because I nailed her in the eyes."

Crossing to the desk, Gideon picked up one of the bottles, holding it up to the light. "So it works just like the obsidian. It can be absorbed through the skin or soft tissue."

"Yes. It's a stronger concentrate than I initially wanted, but I wanted to make sure a little contact would go a long way."

Gideon swore under his breath. "I wish I knew why Henry was doing this in the first place. That would make it a lot easier to predict what move he's going to make next. I think it's a pretty safe bet we're not going to find him at the warehouse again."

"No, no probably not." Jesse leaned forward. "John mentioned unlocking a cage and allowing vampires to rediscover their true natures. But by hiding their so-called true natures, they can live like Rina, or Tricia...or even you. Henry doesn't think vampires should be living with humans, he thinks humans should be...pets."

"Then Henry's an idiot." Gideon resumed his pacing, though his anger was leaking back into his long strides. "I don't blame him for feeling caged, but if he thinks he can control a city full of vamps who just want to chow down on the population, he's got another think coming. They're not going to be satisfied with pets. They're going to want bloodbaths."

"Do you think Henry will shed a tear over the slaughter? It's probably all the same to him. He gets what he wants in the end.

Humans will be gone, or reduced to nothing but slaves, and...if obsidian is addictive, he'll be the center of power." Jesse shrugged. "Of course, that's just what he thinks will happen. If his plan is allowed to continue, another vampire will take him out and fill the power vacuum until he's taken out and so on."

"Which puts us back at square one." Abruptly, he turned on his heel and headed for the door. "How far away did you say you ran into Rina?"

"It was about six blocks south. She was bleeding pretty good, so it should be easy enough to follow her."

That was all Gideon apparently wanted. With a sharp nod, he left the office.

*   *   *

If it had been anyone other than Rina, Gideon would've gone out with the intent to kill. It was one thing to share Jess at Sangre; it was something else entirely for vampires to think Jess was fair game just because they came across him on the street. Jess was his. It was entirely unacceptable for them to treat him as less than he was.

But he wasn't going to kill Rina. She'd run as soon as the antidote hit, Jess had said. It wasn't her fault, but the drug's. Besides, he needed her. She'd already helped him find Tricia. Now it was time to put her to use again and locate Henry.

Her trail was easy to find, the blood still fresh. Gideon broke into a run, following it down a side street and into a squat. He didn't have to go far. She was huddled in a corner in a west-facing room near the front of the building.

Gideon blocked the doorway, arms folded over his chest as he waited for her to notice him. Slowly, Rina lifted her head. Her gaunt features were more pinched than normal, and blood oozed from a scrape at the corner of her eye, but what surprised him was the scent of salt he detected. Her cheeks were dry, but at one point, she'd been crying.

It was even more reason to let her go this time.

"Will you at least make it quick?" she said. Her voice was flat, her eyes even more so. She had already prepared herself for the worst.

Gideon took a step inside, kicking the door shut behind him. Rina flinched at the sharp echo. "No," he said. "This isn't going to be quick at all."

Her lower lip wobbled, but her chin jutted out, the last of her strength surfacing. "He fucking got away! That should count for something."

"He came limping into my office, Rina. You *know* better than that."

"It wasn't me. Did he tell you that? It was that shit obsidian. Trust me, if I hadn't been high, I wouldn't have gone near him. He's not even my type. Shit, he's way too old, for one thing. And he got away. You got him back. Please, Gideon, just give me one more chance."

He didn't move. He didn't blink. He simply waited, to give her the impression that he was actually only now reaching the decision not to hurt her.

Rina broke first, sagging backward as she slammed her head against the wall. "For fuck's sake, Gideon, either do it or don't."

"I won't," he said evenly. Her attention snapped back to him, and he held up a hand in warning. "On one condition."

"Anything. You name it."

It was the only way he could think of to put a stop to this chaos, once and for all. "Get me a meeting with Henry."

CHAPTER 16

There was no need for a valet this time. Instead, Gideon had Jesse drop him off a block away from Sangre and instructed him to stay there as they had planned. He didn't even look back as he strode along the sidewalk toward the club's entrance, but every step closer left him a little bit tighter, his mood a little bit darker. It felt like he had been waiting a long time for this particular meeting.

Trent rose from his stool as Gideon approached, exchanging a nod as he held the door open. Gideon wasn't sure if it was good or bad that the bouncer knew of his appointment. There wasn't time to consider it, though, before Sangre's pulse sucked him in, slowing his steps as he breathed in the musky scent of sex and blood coating the air. Memories of the night with Jess blurred the visions before him until he thought he could actually feel Jesse's ass squeezing around his cock, taste the texture of his skin the second before his fangs split the surface and Jesse's blood flowed over his tongue.

Gideon was hard before he reached the edge of the main floor. It was probably a very good thing he'd left Jess behind.

He spotted Henry right away, balls deep in a double-D blonde. A female vampire was astride the girl's face, but Gideon didn't recognize any of the others who surrounded the scene. There weren't even any of Henry's usual hangers-on lurking nearby. Wending through the crowd, Gideon came to a stop at one end of the couch, putting himself in Henry's sight line if he ever decided to look up from the pussy he was pounding. He wouldn't interrupt. That was the surest way to piss Henry off before they even started talking.

"We don't stand on ceremony here, Gideon," Henry said, without looking up. "Tawnie, get out of Gideon's way."

Tawnie snarled in frustration, but did as she was told, leaving the girl lying there with her cheeks glistening from the juices of Tawnie's pussy. For a moment, Gideon was tempted. His cock ached just from reliving the night with Jess, and coming would take the edge off his mood in order to deal more effectively with Henry. It only took a single glance at the girl's dulled eyes for him to decide against it, though. She might be willing, but she had long ago checked out of the events of the evening. He had no interest in making it worse for her.

"Maybe next time," he said. "There are some things that are a little more important than getting off, don't you think, Henry?"

"No," Henry said, but he stopped and straightened, tucking his erection back into his pants. "But I don't mind delayed gratification." He turned, like he was going to leave the girl, but he paused. "Tawnie," he snapped, "don't touch her."

"But..."

"Leave her alone. None of you touch her until I get back."

Gideon followed Henry around the crowd, ignoring how the girl just lay there even after the vampires dissipated. He had no fears that she would get hurt in Henry's absence; in Sangre, his was an iron fang. Nobody would dare argue for fear of losing their head. It didn't make Gideon feel any better about it, though.

Henry led him through a door marked "Employees Only" and up a narrow staircase. Gideon waited to speak until they were both ensconced in Henry's office, a room deceptively large for Henry's position. A leather sectional filled one corner, but it was the familiar scent of obsidian in the air that drew Gideon's attention. In his pockets, he balled his hands into fists in order to keep his uneasiness at bay.

"You're a hard man to get a hold of," Gideon remarked casually.

Henry gestured at the couch before settling behind his desk. "Really? You could have just picked up the phone, Gideon. I've been waiting for your call."

Gideon weighed his words as he sat down. "Well, you finally got it. I didn't know until a couple days ago that you were the man I was looking for."

Henry pulled a small vial of black fluid from his desk, and set it beside two small glasses. That was soon joined by a decanter of scotch. "Oh? How could I be of service to you?"

"I want to talk about the obsidian. I know you're dealing it. I know you're manufacturing it. And I know it's getting people killed. Now I don't care how you make your money, Henry. What I care about is when my pet gets attacked by some random vamp on the street who's hopped up on your shit. That's not acceptable."

"That sounds like a personal problem, Gideon. I can't be responsible for what vamps do outside of the club. Hell, I'm not even responsible for what they do around here most of the time." He opened the vial and dipped into it with an eyedropper. "But there is a way to keep your pet safe, and get a bit of the action yourself."

Gideon's gaze didn't waver. "Let's hear it."

Henry carefully counted five drops of the inky fluid into each cup. "We all know the influence you have out there." He waved vaguely. "You've got contacts that I don't, contacts that I would love to have. I think we could go far together."

"A partnership. Now why didn't I think of that?" He pretended to ponder the question for a moment. "Oh, yeah, maybe because your boys jumped me the other night when I tried to come see you at the warehouse. Not very conducive to thinking you'd want to play fair, don't you think?"

Henry shrugged, filling each cup with a shot of scotch. "I apologize for that, but they weren't after you. They smelled humans, and we can't have strange people poking around the warehouse. They've been instructed to shoot first and ask questions later, if you know what I mean."

The corner of Gideon's mouth lifted. "I'm a little familiar with that brand of thinking, yeah." He watched Henry rise from the desk and carry the two tumblers over to the couch, holding one out in offering. Gideon took it, but didn't drink right away, instead swirling the golden fluid around in the glass and watching as it darkened with the obsidian. "And what exactly do you want from me in this partnership?"

"Gideon, you used to own this city. It could be yours again. Like it used to be, like it's meant to be. You could have that sort of power again, but this time, it won't take you years and years to secure. In fact, we can do it all in one night. With this." Henry lifted his glass. "I've been releasing the obsidian in trickles, but I think it's time to flood the city."

The light caught the fluid in the tumbler, scattering shards of dark gold across the black leather couch. "That sounds ambitious." He smirked. "That sounds like you might need me after all."

Henry inclined his head. "Drink up, Gideon. We have all night to talk shop."

It took only a moment for him to lift the glass to his mouth, but far more for the scorching alcohol to slide down his throat. Warmth spread throughout his body, followed by a familiar languor, and he smiled at Henry as he held the empty tumbler out.

"I'm used to being in charge, you know. But for you, I'm willing to consider a fifty/fifty arrangement."

"Fifty/fifty is exactly what I had in mind. How do you like that? It's far more powerful than what I sell downstairs. I save the good stuff for private use. But look, if I'm going to keep control of the hordes I'm about to unleash, I need somebody like you. No, I need *you*."

Gideon rose to his feet and began prowling around the room, his darkened eyes drinking in the expensive furniture. A low glass-fronted cabinet near the desk displayed an array of sheathed weapons, all older than Gideon, but he passed by it to head straight for the chair behind the desk.

"You know what I miss about the old days?" He sat down, propping his feet up on the corner of the desk as he leaned back in the soft leather. "Respect. Fledges these days don't appreciate what it means to live as long as we have, Henry."

Henry's mouth twisted in a knowing smile. "No, they don't. They don't understand their own power. It's disgusting out there, Gideon. Being a vampire used to mean something. Humans used to be afraid to walk the streets at night. There was a hierarchy. Now?" He shook his head. "They've never tasted real power...I just want to wake them up."

"Well, I know it worked for me. If it wasn't for your obsidian, I wouldn't have had the balls to fuck Jess the first time." He chuckled. "And we both know how well that turned out."

Henry's smiled widened. "I haven't seen anybody like him around the club for a long time. All the other people that come here...they have this dull look in their eye. Like they've seen so much of the world. They're missing a certain..." He snapped his fingers, like he was looking for a word.

"Purity," Gideon offered.

"Purity, exactly. That's what I liked about your boy."

"That, and his fucking great mouth."

Henry smirked. "Exactly. I heard his ass is better."

"Lemme guess. Eric's bragging." Gideon rolled his eyes. "Only reason I let him fuck Jess was because I knew his needle dick wouldn't stretch him out too much for me later. The bruises he left on the boy didn't even last a day before they started to fade. It was hardly worth the time."

Henry's hand went to his crotch, his pants pulling tight across his erection. "You should bring him around, Gideon."

Swinging his legs off the desk, Gideon leaned forward. "I have a confession to make," he said, his voice low and amused. "You know how you told me to come here alone? Well...I didn't." He jerked his head toward the door. "I left the boy parked in the car down the street. Just in case I didn't like what you said and had to tear your head off. Send one of the boys down to go get him. We'll have a little party." As he grinned, his fangs descended. "I guarantee he'll be the best fuck you've had all year."

Henry ran his tongue over his fangs. "Jeff! Rick! Get in here."

Two large vampires stepped into the room, remarkably silent for their size. They stood with their arms folded, waiting for further orders.

"There's a Ferrari down the street with a treat inside. Bring him here, and don't hurt a single hair. I want him unmarked, do you understand?"

They nodded and slipped out.

"What kind of toys do you have up here?" Gideon's head swiveled around. "I see the knives, but do you have any whips or anything? The boy loves his pain. I swear, you have to hear him scream. You'll come on the spot."

Henry's only response was to cross the room and unlock the closet. The door swung open slowly, revealing a room full of things that'd make Jesse scream for hours.

Gideon ran his tongue over the points of his fangs. "Oh, yeah," he murmured. "Those'll do just fine."

*   *   *

Jesse's part of the plan was to wait, and he found the waiting to be intolerable. What was Gideon doing? Where was he? When should he start worrying? Sweat rolled down his neck and back, gluing his shirt to his skin. His tongue felt swollen. He needed a drink. The twinge in his ankle had faded, but he hoped he wouldn't have to run that night—he wouldn't make it far.

As soon as he caught sight of the two vampires, he knew they were coming for him. They moved with purposeful grace, slicing through the night with each step. Every instinct told him to run. Gideon had left him the keys. He could get far away, out of their reach, hole up somewhere safe and wait for Gideon to return. But these two monsters could be taking him to Gideon—or his death. Or both.

They nearly ripped the door off the hinges, but they were surprisingly gentle with him. He could feel their restrained strength thrumming through their skin, see the dangerous glints in their eyes, but they handled him like they'd handle a kitten, and never said a word.

"Where are we going?"

No response.

"Where are you taking me?"

No response.

"Who are you taking me to?"

No response.

Jess stopped talking, but the fear didn't fade. Especially when they dragged him into the club. They walked him through the throng, and it felt like every single vampire in the room wanted to touch him. They flashed their teeth, growling with hunger. He recognized a few from the last time he was there, and by their knowing leers, he knew they recognized him.

They pulled him up a narrow staircase, and as they pounded on a thick door, Jesse sent a quick prayer into the universe—*please let Gideon be in there*. Before he finished the thought, the door flew open and Henry's strong hand curled around his throat. He yanked him into the room, smashing his throat and crushing his windpipe. Panic flared in Jesse's chest, until he caught sight of Gideon, sprawled out on the couch.

His eyes were black. He looked darkly amused. Jesse jumped as the door slammed behind him.

"What's wrong, boy? Don't tell me you're scared. Henry here's an old friend." Gideon snapped his fingers. "Oh, wait. My mistake. It's not his face you'll recognize."

"Here, let me help." Henry unzipped his pants, freeing his cock. "Know me now?"

Jesse nodded mutely. A vision that had been arousing once before was like a bucket of cold water over his head. Henry's eyes were as opaque as Gideon's, and seeing Gideon like that—all lazy, dark sensuality—would have turned Jesse on any other time.

"We've just been doing some business," Gideon was saying. "And I'm in the mood to celebrate." Nodding to Henry, he waited until the

143

other vampire had relinquished his hold on Jesse's neck before beckoning him forward with two fingers. Jess only took a single step when Gideon said sharply, "On your knees, boy."

Jesse dropped to his knees immediately, knowing that, whether or not Gideon was faking, it was best to follow all the orders without hesitation or question. At least, that was the wisest course if he wanted to survive long enough to figure out just what was going on. He crawled the rest of the way across the floor, coming to a stop once he was eye level with Gideon's knees.

Gideon's hand came to rest on the top of his head. Though his strong fingers threaded through Jesse's hair, there was no force behind it, the touch a soothing caress rather than cruel. Jess was just starting to relax when a sudden yank sent needles of pain through his scalp, and he looked up to see Gideon leering down at him.

"You should see all the pretty toys Henry has," he said. "There's a whip in there that'll strip your skin so fine, it'll take us hours to lay you bare."

Henry stood above him, running his hands down Jesse's spine. "Hours," he agreed, "and that's not all. Floggers, paddles, knives, irons...but there will be plenty of time for that later." He straightened. "Get him naked, Gideon. I think we should share him to seal the deal."

"My pleasure."

Jess had no time to react before Gideon jerked him onto his lap, grinding his erection into Jesse's stomach as their mouths slammed together. The hand that wasn't fisted in his hair slid between their bodies, seeking Jesse's cock, and against his will, he began to harden, responding to Gideon's expert tongue and fingers in spite of his fear.

Gideon paused in mid-kiss, the hand at Jesse's waist stilling. "What's this?" he murmured. He dipped into the near pocket and pulled out a slim bottle of breath spray. With a grin, he held it up for a disrobing Henry to see. "Look at how well I've got him trained. He came prepared to taste all minty fresh for us."

Henry laughed. "He doesn't need to be minty fresh for what I have planned for him."

Jesse barely heard the other vamp, all of his attention on Gideon, and his thumb resting over the top of the bottle. Just a little more pressure, and the fine mist of the antidote would coat the air and fall to Gideon's skin. And Gideon knew it. But he didn't do it immediately. The moment he hesitated seemed to stretch an eternity—just long enough for Jesse to entertain the thought that Gideon was confiscating his only weapon of defense, with no intention to use it at all.

"Open your mouth, Jess."

Jesse did so obediently, but the black eye of the spray bottle wasn't pointed in his direction. Gideon pressed the top down, hitting his own chin and neck.

"Fuck!"

A sharp shove had Jess on his ass, and he looked up to see Gideon glowering above him. His skin glistened from the antidote, but the fury in his eyes looked all too real, and the frissons of fear sharpened their claws in Jesse's spine. Had it worked? If it had, how long would it take?

There was no time to contemplate the answers to those questions before Gideon was hauling him to his feet and dragging him toward a closet door.

"Going to teach you a lesson first," he muttered, yanking it open.

"What the fuck are you doing, Gideon?" Henry's annoyed voice filtered through the open doorway. "I thought we agreed we'd bleed him after."

"I'm just going to make some pretty stripes on his back first," Gideon snapped. He grabbed a vicious whip from the wall, but when his eyes met Jesse's, the opacity of his irises had warmed to their familiar brown. They held gazes for only a second before Gideon shoved him back out into the room. "Get your shirt off, boy."

Jesse unbuttoned his shirt and shrugged it off quickly as Henry moved closer. By the time he was half-naked, Henry was practically on top of him. He was trapped between the solid bodies of the two vampires, and only the brief glance he had exchanged with Gideon kept his heart from jumping right to his throat.

Without warning, Henry grabbed him by the hair and pushed him forward, slamming his face to the desk. "I'll hold him down," Henry announced.

He could no longer see Gideon, but he felt his cool hand slither along his back. "This will make fucking him even better," Gideon said. "I'll do just enough to make the blood drip down his ass."

As Henry chuckled, a deep, malevolent rumble, Gideon stepped away. It left Jess with only the painful grasp of Henry's hand on his head.

The whip cracked.

Jess flinched on instinct, but the sudden realization that he hadn't been hit was followed by the rich laughter of both vamps.

"I love doing that," Gideon said. "Did you see him jump? Fucking priceless."

Jesse bit the side of his mouth to stop the immediate *fuck you*, hot anger washing through him. It at least had the effect of dulling the fear that lingered in his gut and he held onto it.

"Let's see how far he jumps if you get him...right here..." Henry scratched his nails over the small of Jesse's back, aggravating the sensitive skin there, but Jesse didn't think he actually drew blood.

Jesse braced himself for the blow, and the sound of the whip snapped through the room for a second time. But, once again, there was no pain. Just the release of the pressure on his head as Henry's hand fell away.

He glanced up to see the delicate cord of the whip wrapped around Henry's neck. Astonishment was replaced by rage on the vampire's coarse features, but as Jess dove out of the way, Gideon viciously yanked his arm back. It tightened the noose around Henry's throat, slicing through the skin, the flesh, the sinew, until the head separated from the torso.

Both pieces exploded into dust before they hit the floor.

Relief washed through Jesse, turning his muscles to water. Before he could collapse against the desk, Gideon was there, his arm around his waist. Jess clutched his shirt and took a deep, shuddering breath. "God, I was worried that stuff wouldn't work."

"So was I." When his head snapped up to stare at Gideon in disbelief, the vampire shrugged. "Apparently, Henry saves the really strong stuff for his extra special friends. But I couldn't turn him down or he would've known something was up."

Jesse blanched, his stomach turning, his mind turning back to the whip, and the other so-called toys he had only got a brief glance of. "Oh. God."

"It wouldn't have mattered, Jess." Gideon's hand cupped the back of his neck, forcing him to meet his solemn gaze. "I wouldn't have hurt you. I wouldn't have let Henry hurt you. Obsidian strips away defenses so that you act on your deepest desires. What I wanted more than anything tonight was to kill Henry."

Jesse nodded. "I know. I just...didn't really like being put in that situation." He touched his nose, which was still tender from hitting the desk. "It's not swollen, is it?"

"No." Gideon pulled him closer, brushing his mouth across the bridge. "I think I love you even more when you get all pouty like this when you're hurt. Even if it's frustrating as hell."

"I'm not all..." The rest of Gideon's words sank in and Jesse stopped short. Gideon said it so casually, so matter-of-factly that he felt like he missed something. "What?"

Gideon glanced up from where he'd been watching his thumb stroke over Jesse's jaw. "What what?"

"You said you...love me?"

"Yeah." The word came out slowly, like Gideon was gradually coming to the conclusion that he was speaking with someone not as intelligent as he thought. "Haven't I told you that already?"

"No. No, I would definitely remember something like that."

For the first time since uttering the words, Gideon pulled back, visibly wracking his memory. "I could've sworn...well, it doesn't matter. Because I do. Love you." He paused. "I guess I thought you felt the same way."

"I do," Jesse said instantly, vehemently. "I've been...God, Gideon, I've loved you for nearly as long as I've known you."

Gideon immediately relaxed, a small smile curving his mouth. "Good. We're clear then." Reaching across the desk, he picked up Jesse's shirt and shook the vampire dust from it before handing it over. When he spoke again, his tone was teasing. "You need to start paying attention to what I don't say, too. I thought I was being obvious."

Jesse pulled his shirt on stiffly. "Maybe you were being obvious." The pain in his nose, the earlier anger, and the sharp fear of the night was utterly forgotten. "I just never expected...I hoped, but I never expected you to love me, too."

The touch of Gideon's hand to his chest was light, but it stopped Jess from buttoning his shirt. "Why?" Gideon asked softly. His fingers caressed the skin over his heart, every stroke making Jesse's pulse thunder louder. "You're the best thing that's happened to me in...a very long time, Jess. Loving you was probably inevitable."

Jesse knew he could try to explain all the very long nights he spent meticulously explaining to himself why Gideon would never really love him, but that wasn't necessary. His hand went to the back of Gideon's head, his fingers moving through his hair, and he finally kissed Gideon the way he always wanted, not holding anything back or trying to disguise the emotions bubbling to the surface.

Jesse's fingers were tight against Gideon's scalp, and he gripped Gideon's shirt with his other hand, like he was never going to let him go. Gideon wrapped his arms around him in turn, pulling them flush.

Sliding against Gideon's body, Jesse put as much of himself into the kiss as he could. He wanted every inch of Gideon to know him, to know that he couldn't contain his feelings any more.

Jess rarely took the lead when they kissed, but he did now. He controlled the speed, the depth, the delicate dance of their tongues, and the fact that Gideon didn't try to wrest the control back only intensified Jesse's desire. He needed this, after years of silence, and the past two weeks of extreme pleasure—and surrender. He needed to know that Gideon would take it, even if it was just this once.

Flames ignited between their bodies, flaring and spreading everywhere they touched. It would be too easy to stumble over to the couch, to strip Gideon's clothes, to lavish him with attention. He wanted to devote as much energy and time to each inch of Gideon's skin that he was devoting to his mouth, but the last remnant of his self-control kept him from doing that. This wasn't the time, or the place.

When Jess finally pulled away from the kiss, he felt cleansed, as though a storm had ripped through him and abolished all the doubts, the lingering fears, last cobweb strings of reservation. He buried his face in Gideon's neck, struggling to catch his breath and stealing one more moment of contact before they were forced to let each other go and step apart.

"You know we're not out of the lion's den yet," Gideon said, the tone of his voice, more than his words, centering Jesse's attention.

"Right." He brushed the back of his hand over his swollen mouth. "I've been waiting to do that for years."

"You can do more when we get out of here in one piece."

Jess nodded. "Got any ideas?"

Gideon looked around the room, his eyes falling on the swords. "I might."

Jesse smiled and finished buttoning his shirt. He knew they weren't in the clear yet, but the obstacle before them seemed very small indeed. He had never felt so light, so above everything. The vamps outside the door didn't scare him. He hadn't come this far only to lose Gideon now.

CHAPTER 17

Jesse was a silent spectator of Gideon's final meeting with Lucas Richards. They had agreed that the man deserved to know the truth—the whole truth—surrounding his son's death, but ultimately decided that it wasn't in the best interest to reveal it all. Jesse had insisted that Toby deserved his privacy even in—especially in—death, and they settled on a carefully edited version of the truth that would answer all his questions but spare him the more gruesome details.

Jesse watched Gideon like he always did, but now it was different. Now he could watch without fear that Gideon would catch a gleam, an emotion, a moment he wasn't meant to see. Lucas didn't even see him. His attention was also riveted on Gideon, and Jesse might as well been an innocuous piece of art for all the consideration he received from Lucas.

Personally, Jess couldn't wait for Lucas to finally be on his way. He felt guilty about that; this was technically his job. The explanation, the consolation, the soft words of understanding were not Gideon's domain, but Lucas was only interested in what Gideon had to say, and Jesse was only interested in watching Gideon, so it worked out nicely.

When Lucas was finally ready to leave, they both walked him to the door, Jesse following a few steps behind Gideon. As soon as Lucas reached his car, Jesse's hand was drawn to Gideon's back. He rubbed his palm over Gideon's shoulder, and by the time Gideon shut the door, Jess' body was pressed against Gideon's, his lips resting on the back of Gideon's neck. He couldn't help himself.

"We better be even now for the whip scare," Gideon commented. "Because I hate this part of the job."

Jesse smiled. "We're even. But you did very good."

A weary sigh made his shoulders sag. "I think we're going to have to keep an eye out on Lucas. He's not the kind of man to just let things go."

"That's probably not a bad idea. What did you do with Tricia?"

"I bought her a train ticket for New York. Hopefully, she'll take the hint." Stepping away from the door, Gideon retreated to his office with Jess at his heels. He headed straight for the bottle of whisky he kept for schmoozing clients and, without asking, poured out two glasses. "The last thing I want is for Lucas to find her. Toby deserved better than what he got, but it wasn't her fault. Not really."

"I'm sure she's got no reason to hang around here." Jesse sipped from his drink while Gideon downed his. "The fire at the warehouse was on the news this morning, but no foul play is suspected. Nice work."

Gideon sat on the corner of his desk, a mocking smile on his lips. "You say that like I don't always do nice work," he teased. "Don't tell me we're losing the shine already."

Jesse finished his drink and returned the smile. "No, things are still very shiny." As Jesse set his glass down, Gideon hooked his fingers around his belt and pulled him closer. "I could show you how shiny things are."

"Oh?" His nails scraped against Jesse's skin as his hand slipped inside his pants. "And how would you do that?"

Jesse caught his breath as Gideon's fingers brushed against his cock. "I could beg you to tie me up again."

He was surprised when Gideon's hand stilled. "And what if I didn't want to?" Gideon asked, his voice unexpectedly solemn.

Jesse's eyes widened slightly, surprised. "I...I guess I'd ask what you did want to do."

Pulling his hand free, Gideon grasped Jesse's wrist and guided him to his hip, folding his fingers over Jesse's longer ones. "I don't always need the games," he said. "Sometimes, all I want is to be able to sink into a willing partner and have them hold onto me while we fuck." His mouth twitched. "Or, you know, rake their nails down my back because it feels so good. That works, too."

"I can do that," Jesse said, perhaps a little too eagerly. He liked, enjoyed, adored every single thing Gideon did to him, and everything they did together, but he had been longing for the opportunity to do the very thing Gideon described. "Let's do that. Right now."

Gideon laughed, and it dispelled the sobriety that had clouded him. "Am I going to have to give you more lessons in patience?"

He toyed with the buttons on Gideon's shirt. "Probably more lessons wouldn't hurt. We can pencil those in for later."

With a gleam in his eye, Gideon captured Jesse's hand in his and rose from the desk. He didn't say a word as he led Jess out of the office, or on the stairs, or even through his apartment. He didn't speak until they stood in his bedroom.

"You know," he said, turning back to Jesse. His deft fingers tugged at Jesse's belt. "You're probably going to be spending a lot of time here now. More than when we were just business partners."

"Yes, probably," Jesse agreed as Gideon worked his belt free. His hands returned to Gideon's shirt, undoing the buttons quickly and exposing his muscled chest.

Gideon tossed the belt aside and then shrugged out of his shirt before returning to Jesse's pants. "Maybe we should just make it easier for us then and have you move in."

Jesse couldn't speak until Gideon pushed his pants down to his ankles. Gideon wanted to spend more time with him than they already spent together. Gideon wanted to share a bed with him, and let Jesse invade his jealously guarded private life. "I think...that's a really good idea. Are you sure you're going to be okay with that?"

Gideon's eyes danced as he set to work on Jesse's shirt. "I wouldn't have suggested it if I didn't want it. And besides, if you annoy me too much, I'll just throw you in the cage and see if you turn my dream about you jacking off in it into reality."

"That sounds fair enough," Jesse said, unzipping Gideon's pants. He wrapped his fingers around Gideon's erection, but was forced to let him go as Gideon tugged his shirt down his arms. The shirt joined the pants, leaving Jess completely naked, a chill rolling down his back. "But you can probably throw me in the cage even when you're not annoyed."

"I'll think about it," Gideon murmured. His head ducked, and his mouth skimmed over Jesse's shoulder, his tongue like silk where it left a wet trail. "Right now, I just want to taste you all over."

Jesse's heart leapt as Gideon began licking along his chest. He took a path down the middle at first, kissing and savoring before veering to the side and circling around the nipple. Rather than touch it, though, he repeated the caress in the opposite direction, all the while letting his hands knead the tense muscles of Jesse's back.

Jess moaned and let his head fall back as Gideon made good on his promise. His lips were soft, his tongue playful as he lapped at Jesse's skin. His hands were strong on Jesse's back, forcing whatever tension he had out until he could barely stand. He just wanted to slump forward against Gideon, or fall backward to the bed.

It was excruciating when he felt Gideon's skin slide against his as he worked ever lower, but when Gideon dropped to his knees and cupped Jesse's ass, Jess allowed himself the luxury of grasping Gideon's shoulders. He used him for balance as the mouth he had dreamt about for so long lavished every inch of his stomach, but even that attempt failed when Gideon reached down and fondled his smooth balls.

Jesse bent his knees as his thighs tightened, and his stomach clenched with sharp spasms of desire. He knew Gideon could be this gentle and thorough, but it was still a surprise to be on the receiving end of it. Gideon massaged his balls as his mouth moved lower, his tongue sliding along the seam of Jesse's thigh. Jess whimpered, his fingers curling into Gideon's skin.

"I want to suck you," Gideon murmured. His mouth never strayed from the smooth patch of skin at the base of Jesse's cock. "But I'm afraid if I start, I won't be able to stop, and I was kind of looking forward to you coming while I fuck you."

Jesse's breath caught in his throat. "I don't think that'll be a problem. I might not have vampire stamina but..."

Gideon's tongue traced the vein that ran the underside of his shaft. "I'll just have to take that risk then."

Jess gasped when Gideon sucked the head past his lips, stopping to lick away the pre-come that was already flowing so freely. He lingered there for what felt like forever, stroking the sac at the same time, and just when Jess thought he was going to have to beg after all, Gideon moved, sliding down his length. He didn't stop when the tip pushed against the back of his throat. He just swallowed until Jess felt his lips wrap around the root of his cock.

Jesse could only stare at the top of Gideon's head, his breath coming faster and faster. Gideon barely moved, as though he didn't want to lose too much of Jesse's cock when he pulled his head back, but Jesse was panting like he was running a marathon. It was too much, seeing Gideon on his knees like that, feeling his mouth like that, and knowing it was only because Gideon loved him.

Gideon gripped his thighs, and pulled back, sending a slightly chiding look up at him. "Breathe, Jess."

Jesse nodded, took a deep breath and held it as Gideon swallowed his length once again, and let it out slowly.

The lazy rhythm Gideon established carried with it the urge to begin babbling, about how much he loved Gideon, about how he'd do anything for him, about how grateful he was to be able to finally get to share everything he'd always wished. But with each slide into the tight suction of Gideon's mouth came an answering caress along his balls, behind his sac, until Gideon's fingers traced the tight pucker of his ass. Speech wasn't possible then. Especially when Gideon began to hum around his cock.

Jesse touched Gideon everywhere he could reach, his fingers fluttering over Gideon's hair, shoulders, and cheeks. His entire body seemed to be vibrating, pulsing. The pleasure flared, faded, flared, faded, flared again until he was gasping, certain he would burst. Jess didn't know if Gideon was intentionally trying to torment him, if he knew Jess was close to losing it, but he kept pulling Jess away from the brink. Finally, he slid his finger into Jess' ass to press against his prostate.

The shout tore from his lips as his body spasmed, his hips slamming forward of their own accord as he shot deep in Gideon's throat. Blast after blast made him feel like he was ricocheting, and it was only Gideon's strong hands that kept him from falling over. His body trembled, his head spun, and then Gideon was moving, finally releasing the suction around his cock to slide back up Jesse's body and capture his mouth in a hot, sticky kiss.

Jesse wrapped his arms around Gideon, holding him tightly as his body continued to tremble from the force of the orgasm. He smoothed his hands over Gideon's shoulders, down his back, to the waistband of his jeans, still hanging low on his hips. Jess pushed them down, his fingers sliding against Gideon's ass. The kiss went on for a long, long time, Jesse catching snatches of breath when he could. When they finally broke away, Jesse was semi-erect and a fresh, different ache was radiating through his lower stomach.

"I can't believe how much I always need you," Jess murmured.

"And there's another good reason for you to move in." Gideon smiled and pushed him toward the bed, not stopping until Jesse's legs hit the edge of the mattress. "Lie down. I'm not done tasting yet."

Jesse shivered with anticipation and did as he was told, his legs parted, his knees slightly raised. A certain hunger lurked in Gideon's eyes, and Jess shivered again. He kissed him again, but only briefly, just enough to make Jess feel the loss when Gideon moved from his mouth and trailed hot kisses down his body. The tip of his tongue snaked out, wiping across his cock, before moving to the sensitive skin behind Jess' sac.

All he could hear was the roar of his blood as Gideon grasped the back of his thighs and pushed his legs up. It spread his cheeks and exposed his hole, but before he had the chance to grow accustomed to the suddenly cool air, Gideon's mouth covered it, his tongue tracing the entrance his fingers had already explored. Wet, dragging licks made his skin burn, until whimpers began to rise in his throat.

Gideon chuckled. "Do you know that hearing you like this just makes me want to drag this out even longer?" he asked. "I fucking love the sounds you make."

The thought of Gideon prolonging the experience turned the whimpers into a long moan. Gideon responded with another lingering swipe of his tongue, teasing him with the barest hint of a deeper exploration.

"I can't help it..." Jesse said, clutching the bedspread. "I can't help it when you do things like that."

"Like what? This?"

Strong fingers dug into his cheeks, spreading him even wider, and his muscles twitched as Gideon licked over his hole yet again. Jess gasped as Gideon pressed the very tip of his tongue past the tight ring, only exhaling when he retreated almost as quickly.

"Yes, yes. Just like that."

He didn't know if it was his need or Gideon's hunger, but the next wet press against his ass had Gideon's tongue sinking deeper, and the next one after that even deeper yet. Slowly, Gideon fucked him, licking and probing until Jess was quivering uncontrollably, and all he could do was writhe against the sheets.

"Oh my God...Gideon...love this...love you...you feel so good...so good..." Words just kept spilling out, as though he could tell Gideon all about the searing sensation that heated his blood. As though he could convey how much he appreciated every second they were together, and how greedy he was for more, and how at moments like this, he would do, promise, swear to anything.

Gideon pulled back, but the absence of his tongue was replaced by a pair of fingers pushing into his ass. He looked up the length of Jesse's body, his eyes nearly black with desire, and nodded toward the nightstand.

"Get the lube."

Jesse fumbled for the bottle, his fingers slipping once before grasping it. He was trembling by the time he pressed it into Gideon's hands, his ass clenching, his cock now fully erect. Gideon poured a good amount on his fingers before tossing the bottle aside. Jess' eyes were drawn to Gideon's erection, the tip dripping with pre-come, his shaft long and smooth, and he could already feel it sliding into him.

Gideon slid his slicked fingers back inside Jesse's ass, scissoring and stretching for brief thrusts before adding a third and then a fourth finger. It burned in the best way possible, but Gideon didn't torment him for long, removing his hand to slide up the length of Jesse's body. He took Jesse's mouth in a kiss that left him breathless, their cocks rubbing together until Gideon shifted the angle of his hips.

"What do you want?" he murmured against Jesse's lips.

"I want you, Gideon."

He felt rather than saw the slow smile curve Gideon's mouth. Then he felt the blunt tip of his cock pressing past the tight ring of muscle, sinking inch after inch into his ass. By the time he felt Gideon's balls brush against his cheeks, Jess was gulping for air, a situation made worse when Gideon resumed kissing him.

Jesse wrapped himself around Gideon, his ankles hooking around his calves, his fingernails digging into Gideon's back. Gideon deepened the kiss until right at the moment Jesse felt his lungs would explode. But his need for air didn't supercede his need to taste Gideon, and he peppered his jaw and neck with kisses as Gideon slowly slid out of him and then rocked forward.

"I like it like this." The words were a velvet caress, punctuated with the steady thrusts into his ass. "I like seeing how you squeeze your eyes shut right before you come. How you lick your lips when I wait too long to kiss you again."

He turned his head, seeking out the sinew of Jesse's neck, and when his mouth closed over his original bite, sucking gently at the skin, Jess bucked beneath him.

"Oh God..." Jess tilted his head back further, arching beneath Gideon. "I love your mouth, and your cock, and when you're buried in me completely. You feel so good..." Gideon's rhythm was almost enough to turn him completely incoherent, but he pressed on, his words

155

slow and halting. "I'm yours…Gideon…so happy I'm yours."

The growl he heard next vibrated through him, followed by the quickening snaps of Gideon's hips. Blunt teeth worried the small marks on his neck, and then a firm hand found his cock, pulling it at the same tempo Gideon's filled his ass.

Gideon lifted his head a fraction, just enough to give his words room to escape. "Come for me," he said. In the next moment, his fangs sank through Jesse's skin, his cock jerking as his come coated Jesse's slick passage.

Jesse jolted against Gideon, his balls tightening just before he erupted for the second time. Jess expected Gideon to draw more blood from him, but as soon as Jesse's cock stopped twitching, Gideon retracted his fangs and replaced them with his tongue, lapping at the marks until the blood stopped. Jess didn't let him go, his arms and legs still around him, but Gideon didn't seem to mind.

"Love you," Gideon said. He lifted his head, an amused smile curving his mouth. "And see? I can even say it outside of a stressful situation."

Jesse chuckled softly and kissed the corner of his mouth. "I'm impressed. And I promise from now on, I'll do a better job of listening to you."

Gideon snorted. "Like that's ever going to happen. The only way I'm ever going to get you to listen to me is to shackle you to the ceiling again and paddle your ass until it glows."

"Will that be before or after the lessons in patience?"

"Before, during, *and* after." With a grunt, Gideon finally eased out of Jesse, rolling onto his back and taking Jess with him. His arms wrapped around Jesse's back and held him tight, and as Jess watched, his eyes drifted shut. "Thank you."

Jess rested his head on Gideon's shoulder. "You're welcome. For what?"

"For reminding me why I keep on fighting," came the soft reply.

The statement warmed him through to his core, more powerful than any declaration of love Gideon could make. Jess knew he would never doubt Gideon's feelings for him—not after this implicit comparison to the woman who had turned his entire existence around. He now knew exactly what he meant to Gideon, and what they meant to each other. It was almost overwhelming to be loved like that, but Jesse hoped to have a long time to become accustomed to it.

Gideon's breath became increasingly irregular as he drifted to sleep, and Jess pressed his lips against Gideon's neck.

"I'm always going to love you," he whispered, before his own eyes fell shut.

JAMIE CRAIG

Jamie Craig is the pen name used for the collaborative efforts of Pepper Espinoza and Vivien Dean. Both successful authors on their own, they began working together in early 2006. Pepper lives with her husband and cats in Utah, where she attends graduate school, and Vivien resides in northern California with her husband and two children.

*   *   *

**Don't miss *Unveiled*, by Jamie Craig,
available Summer, 2007 at AmberHeat.com!**

Gideon Keel and Jesse Madding have seen dozens of gruesome crime scenes over the years, but nothing compares to the grisly discovery they make in a small apartment above a sporting goods store. The body has clearly been put on display, and clues in the apartment indicate that while she was dying, party guests were enjoying rich caviar and expensive champagne. The two men are mystified.

They receive help from an unexpected source—a young woman they rescue from an auction at the vampire club, Sangre. Emma Coolidge is determined to save her sister from the same monsters Gideon and Jesse are hunting. While both men are utterly fascinated by her beauty, her intelligence, and her rare talent as an empath, they value her for her friendship. The three plan a sting operation to infiltrate the small group of "art connoisseurs" by sadistically turning Jesse into a living work of art, but will it be enough to save the city from more vicious murders in the name of beauty?

AMBER QUILL PRESS, LLC
THE GOLD STANDARD IN PUBLISHING

QUALITY BOOKS
IN BOTH PRINT AND ELECTRONIC FORMATS

ACTION/ADVENTURE

SCIENCE FICTION

MAINSTREAM

FANTASY

ROMANCE

HISTORICAL

YOUNG ADULT

SUSPENSE/THRILLER

PARANORMAL

MYSTERY

EROTICA

HORROR

WESTERN

NON-FICTION

AMBER QUILL PRESS, LLC
http://www.amberquill.com

705896

Made in the USA